'If you marry me then, as your husband, it will be my duty to help you and your family.'

'It's not that—' Put like that, it brought home to Alyse all the more the reason why she should feel this whole deal was just too good to be true. 'It's—what will *you* get out of this?'

Something changed in his blue eyes, as if a wash of dark water was flooding over them, but then, to her astonishment, they cleared again. Dario smiled down into her concerned face, and as he did so he held out his hand to her, palm upwards, as he had done when he had brought back the pearl earring to her the day before. Dazedly she put her own hand into his and felt herself being drawn up to her feet, to stand close to him.

'Do you really have to ask?'

Kate Walker was born in Nottingham, UK, but grew up in West Yorkshire. She met her husband at university in Wales and originally worked as a children's librarian. After the birth of her son she returned to her old childhood love of writing. Her first book was published in 1984. She now lives in Lincolnshire with her husband (also a writer), and two cats who think they rule her life.

Visit the author profile page at millsandboon.co.uk for more titles

OLIVERO'S OUTRAGEOUS PROPOSAL

BY
KATE WALKER

First published in Great Britain 2015
by Mills & Boon, an imprint of Harlequin (UK) Limited,
Eton House, 18-24 Paradise Road, Richmond, Surrey, TW9 1SR

ISBN: 978-0-263-25773-1

Harlequin (UK) Limited's policy is to use papers that are natural,
renewable and recyclable products and made from wood grown in
sustainable forests. The logging and manufacturing processes conform
to the legal environmental regulations of the country of origin.

Printed and bound in Great Britain
by CPI Antony Rowe, Chippenham, Wiltshire

OLIVERO'S OUTRAGEOUS PROPOSAL

For my dear friend Pat
1949–2014
Good friends are like stars…
You don't always see them,
but you know they are always there.

CHAPTER ONE

ALYSE HAD ALMOST given up on her plan, and was on the verge of deciding that the whole thing was a crazy, down-right dangerous idea, when she saw him. She was actually thinking about leaving before this dazzling charity ball had really got started, suffering second and even third thoughts about the wild scheme she had come up with when the crowd before her parted slightly, forming a pathway that led straight from her to the tall, dark male on the opposite side of the room.

Her breath caught, and she knew that her eyes had widened even as she pushed back a fall of golden-blonde hair so as to see him better. He was...

'Perfect...'

The word slipped past her lips, escaping her control and actually whispering into the overheated air.

The man on the far side of the room looked so different, alien almost. He stood out as vividly as a big black eagle in the middle of a bunch of glorious, sparkling peacocks. Of the same species but somehow totally unlike everyone else.

And that difference was what caught her eyes and held them, finding it impossible to look away. She even froze with her champagne flute halfway to her lips, unable to complete the movement.

He was stunning. There was no other word for it. Tall

and strong with a lean, powerful physique encased in the sleek sophistication of formal clothes in a way that somehow made him look dangerously untamed in contrast to the elegant silk suit, the pristine white of his shirt. His tie had been tugged loose at some point by impatient, restless hands, and it now dangled limply around his throat where the top button of his shirt had been wrenched open too, as if he needed space to breathe. The fall of his black hair was worn longer than any other man's there, like the mane of a powerful lion. High slashing cheekbones were etched above the lean stretch of his cheeks, long dark lashes concealing the burn of his eyes as he stared out across the room, the faint smile on his sensual mouth one of cold derision rather than any real sign of warmth.

And it was that that made him perfect. The faint but obvious sign that, like her, he didn't quite belong here. Of course, she doubted that he'd been pushed out into the public world as she had. Her father had insisted that she come here tonight, when she'd much rather have stayed at home.

'You need to get out after spending your days stuck in that poky little art gallery,' he'd said.

'I like my days in the gallery!' Alyse had protested. It might not be the job in fine art she'd hoped for, but she earned her own money and, if nothing else, it gave her a break from the stresses at home when the demands of her mother's illness seemed to throw a black cloud over everything.

'But you'll never meet anyone unless you socialise more.'

For 'anyone' read Marcus Kavanaugh, Alyse thought wryly. The man who had made her life hell recently with his unwanted attentions, his persistent visits and determination to persuade her to marry him. He'd even started turning up at the 'poky little' art gallery so that she had no peace from him. Then just recently, for some reason, Alyse's father seemed to have decided that the marriage would be a match made in heaven.

'He might be your boss's son and heir, but he's just not my type!' she'd protested, but it was obvious that her father wasn't listening. He wasn't actually pressing her to accept Marcus's proposal but, all the same, it was plain that he thought it was unlikely that she'd do better with anyone else.

In the end, exhausted by feeling harassed and oppressed, she'd resolved to come to the ball tonight and use the event as a way to break out of the predicament in which she found herself. Which was where the stranger across the room came in.

Of course, this man obviously wasn't slightly out of his depth like her. His height, stature and the fine cut of his clothes were the match of anyone here, and his expression showed that he wouldn't give a damn what anyone thought of him. Which gave him an added advantage as the necessary partner in what she had hoped for tonight.

Her partner in crime, as it were.

It was as that thought crossed her mind that it seemed it had reached out and touched the man opposite. Because he stirred as if something had alerted him. That leonine head swung round, and his eyes clashed with hers.

It seemed that in the moment her eyes met his the world suddenly tilted, lurching dizzily, so that she actually reached out a hand to press against the wall beside her and keep herself upright.

Danger.

The word seemed to flash wildly inside her head, making her bite her lip in a sort of a panic, but one that was mixed with excitement too. She'd wanted a way to put an end to Marcus's over-persistent pursuit; it would be great if she could have a little fun as she did so. If *fun* was the way to describe the fizz this man put into her body.

She'd started slightly in that moment of fierce contact, jerking her glass so that drops of the pale sparkling liquid splashed out of it, landing on the rich blue silk of her dress and marking it with damp, spreading patches.

'Oh, no!'

She had a tissue in her tiny silver clutch, but reaching for it with one hand while trying to balance the glass with the other only made things so much worse. The delicate stem of her glass flute was clutched between her fingers, the bag almost tumbling to the floor. Her desperate grab to stop it escaping made it slip dangerously in her grasp, slopping more wine onto the tops of her breasts exposed by the scooped neckline of her dress.

'Allow me.'

It was a cool voice, calm and smooth as silk, powerfully soothing. Alyse had barely enough time to recognise that it was deep, masculine and beautifully accented before a pair of hands—long, strong, bronze-skinned—reached out and took the vulnerable glass, the silver clutch from her, depositing them on a nearby table. Then he snagged up an immaculate white napkin and shook it loose before pressing it against her waist, padding at the spill that stained her dress.

'Th-thank you.'

The foolish weakness in her legs was still afflicting her, so she fought for the control she needed. But, in spite of her efforts, she still swayed awkwardly on the ridiculously high heels she was unused to wearing.

'Steady.'

That voice was closer, almost in her ear. Or perhaps that had something to do with the way he had stopped mopping her dry and now that powerful hand had closed around her own, holding her upright.

'Thank you.'

To her relief, her voice was stronger now, firmer, and she felt her balance return. She could stand upright at last, bring her head up, look him in the eye...

And almost lost all that hard-won stability when she looked up into the bluest eyes she had ever seen, deep and clear and bright as a Mediterranean ocean in the sun at the height of the day.

The man who had been on the opposite side of the room now stood at her side, big and dark and disturbing. His tall frame blocked out the light, the sight of everyone else in the ballroom. The heat of his body seemed to reach out to enclose her, and the scent of his skin, mixed with some tangy cologne, was like a warm enchantment all around her so that inhaling it made her head spin in sensuous intoxication.

'You.'

This time she had enough thought left to twist her hand from under his and grab at the strong arm that was near to her. She felt the hardness of bone, the power of muscles bunch and tighten under the silk suit and knew a rush of heat and flame that seared along her nerves, threatening to melt her strength away in the same moment that she rediscovered it.

'Me...' he confirmed, the uneven smile that accompanied the single word strangely ambiguous.

He took the napkin from the hand that still held hers, freeing it for use again.

'Better get this dried off fast,' he murmured, 'before it ruins your dress completely.'

'I—yes...'

What else was there to say? And who else to say it to? It seemed that they existed in a private, closed off bubble, a world of their own while the buzz of conversation went on around her unabated.

That proud dark head was bent, the brush of his waving hair soft against her cheek as he concentrated on the task of cleaning up the mess of wine. He was so close that she felt he must hear the unexpected thunder of her heart, see the way her breathing had sped up, bringing a rush of colour to her skin. That napkin was now moving over the edge of her neckline, crossing the point where blue silk met creamy flushed skin, stroking over the sheen of wine on the tops of her breasts.

It was soft, delicate almost, but in the same second it felt like an invasion, far too intimate for the moment and their surroundings. Too intimate from *him*.

'I think that will do...'

She wanted to spin away, knocking his hands aside, so shaken by the effect his touch was having on her even through the folds of that starched linen napkin. But at the same time she wanted *more* of it. More of that touch and closer, nearer to skin.

So she pushed the response from her mouth, afraid that if she wasn't careful she would replace the words with others. Ones that her primitive female instincts wanted her to throw at him, the words *more* and *please* hovering dangerously close to her tongue.

'I'm fine now—thank you.'

'Yes, I think you are.'

He was still so close that his warm breath stirred the blonde tendrils of her hair where they curled over her ear. But at least his hand had stopped that slow, caressing movement, and he had lifted it from her skin, bundling the napkin into a ball before dropping it back on to the table beside them.

'So perhaps now we can start again.'

The beautifully accented voice had a smile in it, one that was echoed in the curve of his lips. But those deep blue eyes had a cooler, assessing expression in them that made her feel uncomfortably like some specimen laid out on a microscope slide.

'Or, rather, *start*.'

He straightened up fully and it was only then that she realised just how tall he was, the way he had bent to his task disguising the long, lean frame that was approaching three inches taller than hers, even in the four-inch heels.

'My name is Dario Olivero,' he said, holding out a hand in a formal greeting that seemed ridiculous after that enclosed moment of heightened intimacy they had just shared. His voice sounded strangely rough, as if he was speaking from a dry throat.

'Alyse Gregory...'

She followed his lead, her voice almost failing her as she slicked her tongue over suddenly parched lips in an attempt to moisten them, and watched his intent blue gaze drop to watch the betraying movement. She could have sworn that the corners of that beautifully shaped mouth curled up slightly in response and it seemed to her that it was the sort of smile that might appear on the face of a tiger when it realised that the deer it had its sights on was tremblingly aware of its presence.

But even that thought fled from her mind when he took her hand in his and held it, strong and warm and shockingly exciting. It was as if no one had ever held her hand before. At least not with this sizzling burn of contact, the shockwaves of heat that seemed to spread out from every tiny point of contact, burning along her nerves straight to the most feminine centre of her body. The sensations, the thoughts this created felt positively licentious, indecent in such a public place and with someone she had only just met.

They were also the sort of sensations she had never felt

before. Never this fast, this strong, for a man who was almost a complete stranger.

But at least now she knew his name. And she'd heard of Dario Olivero of course. Who hadn't? His vineyards and the superb award-winning wines they created were known the world over.

'Alyse...' he said, and his tone made her name into a very new and very sensual sound, curling the two syllables around his tongue and making them seem almost like a caress. But the look in his eyes still seemed to contradict the soothing sound. The clear dark blue had sharpened, focused strangely just for a moment, then his face relaxed again and he turned on a brief blinding smile.

Alyse Gregory. The name echoed round inside Dario's head. So *this* was Lady Alyse Gregory. He had been told that she was to be at the ball—it was the only reason he had endured the boredom of the evening so far, though it had amused him to watch the other guests, see their false smiles, the air kisses that made no contact, meant nothing at all.

Way back, he would not even have been able to cross the threshold here, let alone mix with this titled and moneyed crowd. If he'd tried, he had no doubt that he would have been shown the door. The back door. A door he'd had plenty of experience of when he'd been in charge of deliveries for the Coretti winery, the place that had given him his first job and set him on the road to success.

Perhaps once he might have been given entry as Henry Kavanaugh's bastard son, if his father had ever acknowledged him. Just the thought brought a sour taste into his mouth. If he had ever hoped for that then tonight the hope was completely erased from his mind. Tonight he was here, accepted, welcomed as himself. As Dario Olivero, owner of the hugely successful vineyards in Tuscany, exporter of the wines that the wealthy and powerful fought to have on their tables at events like this...

A man who had made his own fortune. And of course money talked.

But that wasn't what had brought him here tonight. Instead he'd wanted to meet one woman—this woman.

'Hello, Alyse Gregory.' It took an effort to iron out the note in his voice that revealed the blend of satisfaction and surprise that flooded through him.

He'd expected her to be beautiful. Marcus certainly wouldn't be seen at a huge social event like this with anyone who was less than supermodel material, even if she did have the title that both the Kavanaughs, father and son—legitimate son—believed to be so important.

But this Alyse Gregory was nothing like Marcus's usual run of women. She was tall, blonde, beautiful—that much was true. But there was also something different about her. Something unexpected.

She was far less artificial than the sort of painted sticks Marcus liked to be photographed with. She had curves too—real curves, not the silicone-enhanced bosoms flaunted by Marcus's last but one model of the year. Those moments spent mopping the wine from the creamy skin exposed by her neckline had set his pulse thundering, his trousers feeling uncomfortably tight. The scent of her body, blended with a richly floral perfume, had risen from her skin to enclose him in a scented cloud that made his senses spin. And the moment that a small, glistening drop had slid down into the shadowed valley between her breasts had dried his mouth to parchment so that he had had to swallow hard before he could give her his name.

He was on the verge of making a complete fool of himself, holding on to her fine, long-boned hand for so long.

The smile that had come to her lips was wavering, and he could feel the tension in her fingers as if they were hovering on the edge of being snatched away.

'Forgive me...'

'Hello, Dario...'

The two sentences clashed in mid-air between them, and the sudden release of tension made them laugh, even if a little edgily. When he released her hand he was surprised to see that she still held it up just for a moment, suspended between them, not quite breaking the contact. But a second later she had dropped it to her side again, looking round for the bag he had placed on the table moments before.

'Thank you for coming to my aid.'

'I was coming towards you before that.' He couldn't hold back the truth.

'You were?' Her blonde head went back slightly, green eyes looking up into his face, a small, puzzled frown creasing the smoothness of her brow.

'But of course...'

The smile he gave her now was much more natural, so that he could feel the spark of awareness in her before her own lips curved in response.

'And you knew it.'

'Did I?'

She was going to back away from it; the sharpness of the question told him that. That, and the sudden lift of her chin in defiance, the firming of that full, sensual mouth. She was going to deny that stunning, fiery spark of awareness that had flashed across the width of the huge room in the moment that their eyes had met. An awareness that had pushed him into action, moving towards her before he had even recognised what was happening or stopped to think, in a way that was totally out of character. He was not the sort of man who acted on impulse; he never made a rash move. Everything was thought out, the last detail finalised—'i's dotted, 't's crossed. He was known for it. It was what he'd built his reputation—and his fortune—on: that total focus, the white-hot attention to detail.

And yet here he was, standing before a woman he had seen from across the room, simply because he had been unable to do anything else.

He didn't even have the excuse that she was the woman he'd come here looking for. When he'd taken those first steps to her side he'd had no idea that she was Alyse Gregory.

That feeling had been in her too. He had seen it in her face, in the way she had choked on her wine as she'd tried to swallow it. He had been so totally sure...

'Did I?' she challenged again.

Those green eyes dropped from his, glancing swiftly to her right, to the huge archway where, even this late in the evening, a steady stream of new arrivals were making their way into the overcrowded ballroom. She must be looking for a way of escape, and irritation at the thought that her cowardice would make her deny the truth started to prickle over his skin.

But then, unexpectedly, she paused, turned back, lifted her head again.

'Yes, I did,' she said, strong and firm and almost bold. 'And if you hadn't, then I would certainly have come to you.'

It was such a turnaround that he felt almost as if the world tilted on its axis and something happened so that the woman he had first seen had disappeared and been replaced by another one. Identical in appearance but so very, very different.

'So come on then,' she teased, a new light in her eyes. 'What were you heading towards me for?'

Good question. And one that he was damned if he could answer, with his brain suddenly turned to mud, while the more basic response of his body threatened to scramble his thoughts.

It was just his damned luck that the Alyse Gregory he had come here looking for was the sex kitten who had looked at him across a crowded room, their eyes connecting in an instant lightning strike, calling to him wordlessly with a come-hither glance. And now that he was here…

At that moment, out of the corner of his eye, he saw a movement on the stairs, a sleek blond head he recognised instantly. Marcus had finally made his appearance. Reminding him that the whole point of this had been to make sure that Marcus's scheme to present his father with a titled daughter-in-law came off the rails before the night was over. Time to go back to plan A. Though, if he was lucky, he could put the new plan B into action at the same time.

'I wanted to ask you to dance.'

Now, which woman would answer him? Which Alyse Gregory would give him a response—and in what sort of mood?

'Of course.'

It was another Alyse entirely—a brand new one and one that was totally disconcerting. That smile would have lit up rooms, rivalling the huge glittering chandeliers in the high ceilings of the ballroom. And yet there was something odd about it, something that did not quite ring true. It was *too* bright, *too* blinding.

Too much.

But if that was what she was going to offer then he was going to take it. It fitted with what he had planned. Hell, it fitted with what he *wanted*, and he was having a hard time remembering what he'd planned when what he wanted was beating at the inside of his head like a pounding headache.

'I'd love to dance.'

She held her hand up towards him, and what could he do but take it? They turned towards the dance floor, made their way into an open space. They had just a few moments of the light-hearted waltz that was being played. Enough time to take up the correct position, his arm at her waist, and, as soon as they had, the dance came to a halt, the music stopped.

'Well...'

Alyse laughed, slanting an amused glance at their still linked hands, the careful positioning of their arms. But she didn't make any move to turn away, to break his hold. Instead she stayed where she was, eyes the bright green of purest emeralds as she looked up into his face.

'I still want to dance...'

Dario didn't give a damn about the dancing. But if it meant that she stayed here like this, hands touching, close to him, so that he could see the rise and fall of her breasts as she breathed, watch the colour come and go in her cheeks, inhale the warm soft scent of her body as it came up to him with his head bent down towards hers, then he wasn't going to be the first to break away. So he stayed where he was and waited.

Luckily the next dance was another waltz and, after a couple of seconds counting the beat, Alyse launched into the steps, swaying sensuously, taking him with her. She was incredibly light-footed, barely seeming to touch the floor as she drifted over it.

I still want to dance...

Her own words echoed inside Alyse's head, but she hardly recognised them for what they were. In that moment she had felt as if her mind was suddenly assailed by a multitude of sensations, buzzing and fizzing through her thoughts.

She hadn't just wanted to dance. She had been overwhelmed by an uncontrollable hunger to dance with this man. To feel his hand in hers, his arms around her. And it had nothing to do with the idea that had been in her mind when she had first seen him. The wild plan to find someone who would help her put Marcus off. Who would—hopefully—stop his intent pursuit of her when nothing else had worked.

But this had nothing to do with that. It had only and everything to do with Dario Olivero and the man he was. The man who had knocked her off balance from the moment she had first seen him and from then it felt as if her mind was not her own.

'Dario...' She tried out his name, feeling it as strange on her tongue, catching on her lips. But it was swallowed up in the melody they were dancing to. 'Dario...' she tried again, louder this time.

The dark head bent, blue eyes connecting with hers, searing off a protective layer of skin so that she felt everything—every touch, every movement, the warmth of his breath as it stirred her hair with a new and shocking intensity. She didn't know how she moved her feet, only managing to keep to the steps of the dance by pure instinct as her gaze locked with his.

'You dance very well...' she managed, a tumble of words over a tongue that was thickened with tension and awareness. 'More than well,' she added and felt rather than heard the rumble of laughter in his chest so close to her ear.

'It's a bit late to realise that,' he teased softly. 'What if I had two left feet and trampled you underfoot from the moment we started?'

I wouldn't have minded. She had to clamp her lips shut fast to stop the words escaping from her unguarded mouth. She didn't feel as if her feet belonged to her anyway. She could almost have been hovering six inches above the floor, her steps so light and beyond her control.

'Then relax.'

'I am relaxed.'

He didn't respond—at least not verbally but the slow lifting of one dark brow to question her comment made her heart kick in stunned reaction. Her mind might be whirling in sensation, but her body was holding itself straight and upright as she had been taught in the dance classes her mother had insisted on at the exclusive school she'd attended. The distance between their bodies was tiny—barely there.

But then she looked up into those stunning blue eyes and her heart skipped a beat. There was so much less of that blue there now, the enlarged black of his pupils swallowing up all the colour until his gaze was like a lake of black glass in which she could see herself reflected, small and so very vulnerable. She lost time for a moment, and almost stumbled. She might have tripped if it hadn't been for the strength of the arms supporting her, the width and power of the broad shoulder under her hand.

But it wasn't vulnerability that made her heart kick so hard under the blue silk of her dress that she had to catch her breath on a hasty gasp. It was a realisation that made her head spin, her pulse race.

He felt it too.

She could hardly believe it but there could be little doubt it was true. Dario Olivero, the dark, dangerous-looking pirate who just minutes before had been a total stranger, was now in the grip of the same heated response that was burning her up like a bush fire. He was as aroused as she was, and she was close to swooning with need, weakened by the sort of sensual hunger that she had never known before.

'Dario...'

This time his name was just a croak, the dryness of her mouth, her throat making it almost impossible to speak. But he caught it and a strange flicker of a smile curled the corners of his sensual mouth before he bent his head again and let his cheek rest against the side of her head, his lips brushing her hair as he whispered one word again.

'Relax...'

Gently but irresistibly he drew her towards him, the pressure of one powerful hand tight against her back, the heat of his palm burning the exposed skin over her spine.

'Relax...' he repeated, the softly accented voice entrancing her.

She melted against him, her body curving against his, loose and pliant. Her head was against his chest so that she could hear the heavy, strong beat of his heart under her ear. The scent of him enclosed her, the sway of her body matching his, and she gave herself up to sensation, to an awareness and sensitivity that swept aside the possibility of any other feeling. The heavy pressure of his arousal against her stomach awoke an answering hunger deep inside, an ache of need that was both pleasure and a yearning that demanded to be assuaged.

But not yet. Not until she had enjoyed this sensation of closeness, this connection for a while longer, and taken from it all she could get.

He had a nerve, Dario told himself, telling her to relax, when all the time his whole body felt as if it was in the grip of a raging fever that threatened to burn him up, reducing any chance of control into a pile of ashes blowing round his head. The fact that she had obeyed him only added to the tautness of every nerve that stung with tension every time she moved.

The whisper of her soft soles on the floor, the swirl of the bright blue dress around her slender legs all worked on his senses with hypnotic effect. Every sense, every part of him, his whole concentration was on the woman he held in his arms—the feel of her, the scent, the touch of her against his hands, skin against skin. But it was not enough. He wanted more and yet he was not prepared to stop this, to have it end. Not yet, even if it was to move on to something more viscerally satisfying. Something that every cell in his body was starting to demand with hungry determination.

This wasn't what he had planned on, what he had expected to happen. But right now he was more than prepared to let it go its own way. Any thought of thwarting Marcus's plans had been relegated to the hazy part of his mind. He would let this play out as it was for now...

He drew in a sharp, controlling breath just as one song came to an end and the band began another one. A slow dance. The sort of dance that encouraged a man to take a woman in his arms and hold her close.

So had he made the move or had Alyse stepped closer, moving into his arms without hesitation? She was so close, curved against him, the arch of her body pressed against his at breast and waist and hip so that it was impossible that she couldn't feel the heat and hardness of the hunger he was unable to disguise. She must feel it and yet she showed no sign at all of objecting. If anything, she slid a little closer, making him curse silently at the pleasure that was so close to pain that burned through him as a result.

'Alyse...'

It was just a groan, a note of warning. A public gathering, an elegant ballroom, was not the place for a response like this—so hard, so hot, so strong. This was a sensation that belonged in the bedroom, with his clothes flung wildly aside, the blue silk ripped from her body. It was all he could do to rein his raging senses in, hold himself upright...

'Oh, hell...'

It was impossible. Couldn't be done.

With an acknowledgement of defeat, he dropped his head down low, brushing his lips against the golden silk of her hair, feeling the delicate strands slide under his mouth. She murmured something softly and moved just a little closer, angling her head against the support of his chest so that the fine skin of her cheek, her neck, were exposed, offered to him for the kiss, the caress he knew he could not hold back from taking.

The taste of her flesh was like a drug, intoxicating, seducing him. He couldn't wait any longer.

'Alyse...' His voice was rough and thickened with passion against the delicate curve of her ear. 'I want... Let's...'

'Let's go somewhere else.' Her voice blended with his, the words exactly the same. The same note of hungry need blurring the sound so that they swirled and spun inside his head. 'Somewhere more private.'

When she disengaged herself from his grasp and her hand slid into his, curving soft and warm around his fingers, Dario had no idea whether he was the one who took them from the dance floor or if in fact it was Alyse who led the way.

He only knew that this had been inevitable from the moment their eyes had first met. It was written into their fates, and no one and nothing was going to stop this now.

CHAPTER TWO

THE HALL BEYOND the ballroom was silent, strangely unoccupied after the crowds that had packed the other room. A buffet supper was being served as part of the event, and many people were already queuing there, waiting to be served. As a result, the almost empty hallway seemed unexpectedly cold and uncomfortable, making Alyse shiver in shock at the sudden change of temperature.

'I need my coat...'

She fumbled in her clutch bag, looking for the cloakroom ticket. She had just found it when Dario reached over and took the slip of paper from her hand with a sharp tug.

'Wait here.'

A gesture of courtesy—or taking control? Alyse couldn't help wondering as she watched him stride across the marble floor to where the cloakroom attendant stood on duty. She didn't know and she didn't want to stop and consider the question. *Control* was a word she associated with her father—or with the sort of behaviour Marcus had been trying to force onto her—and she didn't want to think of either of them right now.

Just two minutes out of the ballroom—two minutes away from the warm and intimate closeness of their dance—and already the heat and sensation had started to evaporate, leaving her with an uncomfortable shivery feeling inside. She wrapped her arms around herself in a vain attempt to bring some warmth back to uncomfortably chilled skin.

She hadn't wanted to move apart from him; hadn't wanted to break out of that cocoon that had formed around them. From the moment they had moved, Dario turning away from her, a cold, creeping sense of reality had started to invade the little bubble of delight she had been living in.

'What am I doing?'

She actually muttered the words out loud as she kept her eyes fixed on the back of Dario's dark head, the width of his powerful shoulders.

Was she really planning on heading out of here with him? With a man she had only met...her eyes slid to a clock above the cloakroom door...less than an hour before.

The main door opened with a heavy swish, someone who had gone outside for a sneaky cigarette coming in and leaving it partially open. Alyse balanced on her toes like an athlete readying for the gun to sound the starting point. She could go now...

But even as she took a step forward she caught the wave of cold and damp that came into the hall from behind the new arrival. His jacket was splashed with water too, warning of a change in weather outside. She would need her coat...and her coat...

Was in Dario's hands, the fine black velvet looking impossibly soft and delicate in the grip of those long, tanned fingers.

She couldn't get her feet to move, freezing where she stood, her eyes locking with his over the heads of the people around them. He knew what she had had on her mind; she could tell it from the faint fast frown that drew those dark brows together, the narrowing of the blue eyes.

'Helena!'

Behind her, just beyond the doorway into the ballroom, Alyse heard an uncomfortably familiar male voice raised in greeting and just the sound of it brought a rush of a whole new set of feelings. In the space of an uneven heart-beat she was brought back to the moment she had arrived at the ball, the desperate plan, only half formed, to make sure that Marcus saw her with someone else so that then perhaps he would take no for an answer.

A swift sidelong glance over her shoulder brought con-firmation of the slow creep of unease down her neck. Mar-cus was here. Suddenly, from wanting him to see her with someone else it had become the last thing she wanted. She wanted to get out of here now and let this evening that had suddenly turned magical in contrast to weeks of tension and strain continue. Pushing herself into action, she turned her feet towards Dario.

'Thank you.'

It sounded as if she had run up a flight of steps rather than across the smooth marble tiling.

'I'm going to need this…' She was already pushing one arm into a sleeve of her coat as she spoke, manoeuvring herself so that she could hitch it up over her shoulder. 'Have you seen the weather outside? It's pouring with rain.'

The shiver she affected was meant to be in response to the conditions outside but it was given an added edge by the worrying sense of unease as she saw the way his gaze went over her head, skimming the entrance hall as if looking for someone.

Automatically, his hands came out to help her pull the other sleeve over her arm, lifting the fall of blonde hair from her shoulders and smoothing it down over the black velvet.

Hurry—hurry! Alyse urged him in the silence of her

thoughts. *Please, let's get out of here before Marcus intervenes.*

'We'll have to get a taxi...' she said, pushing her arm under his and curling her hand around the strength of bone and muscle under the fine silk of his jacket. 'Or we'll get soaked.'

She was almost tugging him on his way, urging him towards the door.

'No need,' Dario muttered, nodding towards the uniformed man who held a large black umbrella that he had fetched from a nearby stand above their heads, protecting them from the lashing rain.

'Your car, sir...'

The sleek black vehicle had come to a growling halt at the kerb, the back door opened for Alyse to make her way under the protection of the umbrella. She had only just slid into place on the soft leather seat when the door was slammed after her, and Dario made his way swiftly to the other side. An instant after that, the chauffeur, obviously needing no instructions as to their destination, put the car into motion as he pulled away from the kerb.

Alyse's mood seesawed again, taking her from a need to escape to another, even more unsettling feeling. One that left her breathless and suddenly cold, in spite of the warmth inside the car. Dario's fixed determination had disturbed her so that she could almost believe that she had been kidnapped, taken against her will.

And yet she knew she had been a party to it. More than that, she had been so swamped by the response of her senses that she wasn't thinking straight. She had been burning up with hunger, the sensual need that had uncoiled in the pit of her stomach and radiated out along every nerve. If they could have moved *then*, been instantly transported from the ballroom to wherever they were going, then she wouldn't have had a moment to think, to allow any hint of second thoughts to slide into her mind.

But now, when it seemed that the cold of the evening was seeping into her bones, a slow sneaking sense of apprehension destroyed that wonderful heated knowledge that this was *right*. That it was what she had been looking for all her life. The restrictions she'd had to put up with in order to help care for her ailing mother had limited her chances for the sort of fun and spontaneity her friends enjoyed. Tonight was going to be so very different.

Twisting in her seat, she glanced back the way they'd come, the brilliantly lit doorway to the hotel shielded from the rain by the canopy that flapped furiously in the wind. The weather had driven almost everyone indoors so there was only the doorman on duty. But as she watched a single figure emerged from the hotel doorway and stood, feet planted firmly apart on the red carpet, his whole body turned in their direction, his gaze obviously following the progress of the car as it sped away. The lamplight gleamed on the bright red-gold of his head, making it plain just who he was. He couldn't be anyone else.

Marcus Kavanaugh. The man whose single-minded campaign to bully her into marrying him had blighted her life for the past few weeks. She had done everything she could to make it plain that he meant nothing to her, but it hadn't worked. Of course she'd had to be polite. He was her father's boss's son after all. But politeness hadn't worked. And now that her father had joined in the campaign to see them married, insisting it was the match of the century, she'd felt hounded, trapped, driven into a corner.

It was the memory of how the other man had behaved this morning that made her shudder faintly. She could still hear Marcus's voice telling her that she would regret it if she gave him the runaround any more, and some dark edge to it had made her blood run cold. It was that that had pushed her into the plan she'd had for tonight.

Hastily, Alyse turned back, huddling into her coat.

'Cold?'

Dario's enquiry sounded innocuous but there was an edge to it that brought her eyes up to his in a rush, wary green meeting assessing blue.

'You shivered,' he pointed out.

'Did I?' The inanity of the conversation brought home to her the strangeness of the situation she was in. It was the sort of overly polite small talk you made with a complete stranger when you had just met for the first time.

But that was what Dario was. A stranger. A tall, dark, devastating stranger, and yet a man she had connected with from the start. One whose touch had lit a fire inside her when he'd held her on the dance floor. A man who had driven all thoughts of common sense or self-protection from her head when he had whispered, 'Let's go somewhere else…' in the same moment she had used the exact same words.

Could this be real? She couldn't have this sort of connection in so short a time. And yet this was what she had planned on happening all along. This was supposed to be her get-out-of-jail-free card, wasn't it?

Once more, she made herself look back over her shoulder, seeing the blond man raise his hand to hail a taxi as the car turned a corner and he disappeared from sight. She couldn't hold back a smile at the thought that, no matter what else happened, at this moment Marcus was very definitely out of the picture. The rush of the sense of freedom to her head was like the effect of strong alcohol.

'Feeling better?'

He'd caught the smile—that much was obvious—and wanted an explanation for it. She was never going to tell

him the real truth—but then that truth had nothing to do
with him. Just as what happened from now on had nothing
to do with Marcus. The result was the same, but the one
thing she hadn't expected when she'd come up with the
whole crazy plan was how much she had *wanted* to do this.

'I could feel even better,' she murmured, sliding over the
seat and moving closer to the big, lean body of Dario Olivero. Wanting, needing his arms around her again. 'Yes,'
she sighed as the heat from his closeness thawed some of
the chill of apprehension inside her. 'Like that.'

He couldn't see her face, Dario reflected as she rested her
head against his chest. But the faint purr in her words told
him it would still be there on her lips. She felt like a small
cat, curled up close, the blonde silk of her hair brushing
his chin, the aroma of her perfume swirling around him,
making him inhale deeply to draw in more of it. Held as
close as she was, she couldn't be unaware of the heat and
hardness of his body, the way his heart kicked up at every
move she made so that it was almost impossible to keep
his breathing steady and controlled. When her head tilted
slightly upwards towards his, he knew that she wanted him
to kiss her. But not now, not yet.

'We'll soon be there,' he told her, the swift sidelong
glance towards the chauffeur meant to imply that they
needed to wait until they were alone. And that was definitely true. But there was more to it than that.

He wanted to know what that smile had meant. And why
it had appeared on her lips, warming her expression, just
after she had looked back through the car window. There
had been nothing there to make her smile. Only that one
glimpse of Marcus.

And Marcus was nothing to smile about.

Dario's own smile, reflected in the black glass of the

window, was grimly triumphant, the flash of lights as they passed showing up the cold curve of his lips, the determined set of his jaw. Marcus had lost this round—and, with any luck, the rest of the contest.

'Just round this corner.'

And, as he spoke, the car swung round the bend, sending a spray of dark rainwater up over the kerb from a puddle that had gathered as a result of the storm. A short way down the road, they pulled up outside the building where his newly bought apartment took up the whole of the top floor.

'We're here,' Dario urged Alyse, his tone suddenly rough with the knowledge that if he didn't get her out of here and up to that penthouse *fast* then what little was left of the control that had been fraying mercilessly with every sway and pitch of the vehicle that brought her slender warmth even closer to him would snap completely. He would have to have her under him, his hands plundering her soft curves, her silken skin, and to hell with the audience of José the driver or anyone else.

'Time to get inside...'

The image of being inside her that the words flung into his brain was almost his undoing. He grabbed at Alyse's shoulders, wrenching her up from the half lying, half leaning position before he claimed her hands. Folding his around both of hers and pulling her along with him, he exited the car backwards, not even flinching as his broad shoulders met the force of the wind, the slash of the icy rain that was splattering down over his head.

'Come on.'

He pulled his jacket up high to cover her head like an improvised umbrella, protecting that silky hair from the onslaught of the downpour.

'José, I won't need you any more tonight...'

He tossed the command at his driver as he slammed the car door shut behind them, not needing the man's nod of agreement—or the knowing smile that said his employee had already recognised that fact before they'd arrived.

It was like travelling blind, Alyse reflected, her eyes not quite focusing in the glare of the brilliantly lit building after the darkness of the night. She knew that she was crossing a highly polished floor, heard Dario speak some greeting to the man at the desk as they passed, and then they were at the polished steel entry of a lift, the doors sliding open immediately in response to his long bronzed finger pressed on the call button.

So she had to be grateful for the curve of his arm around her. It felt safe and supportive there, the heat and scent of his body enclosing her, and it was as if that warmth was melting away the worries, the apprehension she had felt at first in the car. Now she felt her limbs soften, leaning towards him, resting her head, her weight against the power of his body. The clean scent of his skin surrounded her, blended with some sort of lime cologne, and she gave herself up to the delight of the physical sensations she was experiencing.

'Alyse...'

His tone was soft, slightly roughened at the edges. She lifted her face, her eyes connecting with his, seeing the intense darkness of his pupils, the tiniest edge of blue around their rim. For a moment she was held, mesmerised, unable to look away, and instinctively her lips parted, a faint sigh escaping to blend with his hot breath as his mouth descended towards hers.

His kiss was warm, slow, infinitely seductive. It took her mouth in a wave of languorous delight, lifting her up onto her toes to wrap her arms around his neck, tangle her fingers in the black silk of his hair. The arm that was curled around her shoulder tightened sharply, drawing her closer, bringing her up against the hardness of his body. Lean, strong fingers stroked down the delicate skin of her neck, slipping under the collar of her coat, making her shiver in need. Her heart rate kicked up sharply, sending her blood pulsing through her body, so that she wriggled even closer in burning awareness.

He felt the same, she could tell. There was the undeniable evidence of the hard swell of arousal pressed into the bowl of her pelvis, the faint groan that escaped from between their joined lips before he brought his mouth down harder, stronger, crushing her lips back against her teeth.

'Dario…'

Somehow she choked it out, not wanting to lose the pressure of his mouth on hers. He tasted wonderful, and the moment that his tongue slid over her lips, tracing the seam where they joined, had her sagging against him, losing her breath, losing all sense of where she was.

Would the lift never reach its destination? She wanted to be there—somewhere, as Dario had said, they could be alone together, private, intimate. Yet at the same time she didn't want this moment to end. She wanted to go on and on for ever in this warmth and closeness.

But even as the thought crossed her mind the compartment jolted slightly, came to a halt, throwing her off balance and right into Dario's arms as the doors slid open again.

'We're here.'

Somehow he managed to ease his keys from his pocket and unlock the door while still holding her close, never easing his grip on her arm, her waist.

In spite of the darkness it was obvious that the room was huge, no light illuminating it other than the reflection

of the buildings and the streetlamps far below. The faint
gleam of the heavy swell of the river was like a silver rib-
bon, and over to the left the ethereal spider web of a blue
circle that looked impossibly delicate to be the London Eye.

She barely had time to adjust to the change in light or
look round any more before Dario had tossed his jacket
away to the side, heedless of whether it landed on a nearby
chair or not, and reached for her again.

'Come here,' he muttered, his voice rough, his accent
thickening on the words. 'I've been waiting—wanting to
do this ever since the moment I saw you.'

His hands were clamped around her shoulders, rough
and bruising, but Alyse neither fully registered it nor truly
cared. All that mattered was the passion of that beautifully cruel mouth on her lips, on her skin, the pressure of
the hard frame of his chest crushing her breasts. The heat
of him surrounded her, flooding her body along with the
burn of her own arousal until she was astonished that the
pair of them didn't go up in flames.

'I—I—yes...'

It was all she could manage, all she could snatch in, in
the moment he allowed her to breathe before his mouth
took hers again. His hands closed over her arms as he
swung her round, half walking, half carrying her towards
the shadowy shape of a huge dark sofa. Her shoes slipped
from her feet as he lifted her up, left behind on the soft
carpet as his right hand reached round to the back of her
neck, finding the zip at the neckline of her dress, swiftly
and expertly tugging it down. The release from even the
slight constriction of her clothing was like a rush of release to her feelings. Inside the delicate lace of her bra,
her breasts stung, pressing against the soft silk, seeming
to demand the attention of those strong, rough-palmed
hands, and she moaned her encouragement as he stroked

his powerful fingers down her body, making her writhe upwards to meet his touch, wanting it stronger, harder. Wanting more.

Then she was lying on her back on the settee, the soft buttery leather cool against the skin that his hands had exposed. And Dario was coming down on top of her, the heavy heat of his skin, the weight of his frame crushing her back into the cushions. One long, finely trousered leg pushed between hers, easing them apart so that she could feel the swollen heat of him pressing against her, crushing into her pelvis, coming so close to the throbbing core of her femininity where the bite of primal need fought against the restriction of their clothing.

'Dario...'

She was reaching for his hands, wanting them on her, wanting to place them where she needed his touch most. She was trying to draw them down to her yearning flesh, but at the same time she wanted to reach for *him*, hungry for the heat of his skin, the taste of him hard upon her mouth.

'I want—I wa...'

But her scrambled words were halted, all train of thought shattered by a sudden violent sound. Someone was at the door, banging hard and slamming a fist against the wood until it seemed that it might actually shatter under its force.

'What?'

Braced hard against the leather settee, Dario froze, his whole body stiffening, his dark head coming up, slightly cocked towards the door, listening intently.

'Who?' Alyse whispered, but he stilled her with a glance, laying one finger across her mouth to silence her. And now, although the scent of his skin was so very close, when all she had to do was to open her mouth and take him in, taste the intensely personal flavour of him as she had wanted just moments before, it was suddenly the last thing she could do. The last thing she dared to do until she knew who had intruded on their seclusion, blasting their way into the heated intimacy they had created and threatening to destroy it totally.

'Olivero!' Another bang at the door clashed with the darkly furious use of Dario's name. 'Open this door, damn you! Open it now!'

A slight gleam in the moonlight showed how Dario's eyes slanted once, briefly, towards where Alyse's head rested against the leather-covered arm of the sofa, then swung back again in the direction of the door.

'Open this door, you bastard! I know you're in there— and Alyse with you too.'

'No!'

The word escaped Alyse in a panic as she recognised the sound, even though distorted through the wood. She knew just who was on the other side of that door, and the fury in his tone reminded her uncomfortably of his threatening warning earlier that day.

'Olivero, you coward, come out and face me...'

'Dario—no!'

Alyse's cry was drowned by another slam of a heavy fist against the wood, and as she reached for him Dario was already levering himself up and off her, that last insult clearly too much for him to take.

Not troubling to rake a hand through his disordered hair or even to smooth down his rumpled clothing, he was striding towards the door, twisting the handle with a violent movement and yanking it open ferociously.

'Well?'

The momentary silence that greeted his appearance, the angry demand of his single word, made Alyse's skin crawl, a cold slimy trail of apprehension sliding down her spine. From where she lay she could see the door, and the man who stood on the other side of it. She had been right, as she knew she'd had to be. The red-gold hair, clashing painfully with a furious scarlet face, the blazing blue eyes were unmistakable. The furious intruder was Marcus Kavanaugh.

But what was he doing here? And how?

He had seen them leave the hotel, had watched them drive off together. She had seen him staring after them when she had looked back through the rain. But how had he known just where to find them? He wouldn't have had time to catch a cab and trail them to Dario's apartment, so how had he known to come straight here and to catch them...?

'Alyse...'

Marcus had turned his attention to her now and, with a small sound of horrified embarrassment, she scrambled up from her place on the settee, forcing herself to her feet. She might have wanted him to get the message—but not like this.

'What the hell are you doing here?'

'I would have thought that was obvious.'

Marcus's spluttering blaze of fury was bad enough, but the edge of laughter in Dario's retort was far worse, setting her teeth on edge and bringing home to her just how dreadful this must all look. She had been sprawled on the settee, her hair tumbling down around her face and shoulders, her legs wide apart, and her clothes...

Cheeks flaming, she tugged her skirt down, struggled to pull her dress up around her shoulders once again, desperate to restore her appearance to a degree of order. Her hands shook so badly that she couldn't reach the zip to pull it up and when she tried to draw Dario's attention to the fact, telegraphing wildly with her eyes and her brows that she needed help, his only response was a blank-eyed stare. Either he didn't understand or…

Her heart quailed inside her, her stomach turning over in sudden nausea. Was it possible that Dario knew only too well what was troubling her but had no intention of making any move to help her? It certainly looked that way. He had barely spared her a glance; instead, all his attention was focused on his raging adversary.

'I— This isn't what you think, Marcus…'

She stumbled over the words, lost them completely when she saw the way that Dario turned, casting a darkly contemptuous look in her direction as if he could barely believe that she had actually said such a stupid thing. Listening to herself as the idiotic comment hung in the air between them, she couldn't believe it either. There was only one possible interpretation of the scene in front of Marcus, and that was the right one. It had also been the one she had wanted him to have, but that had been before this dark fury had erupted around her—and before Dario had seemed to turn away from her.

'And what the hell else would I think it might be?' Marcus spat at her now, making her flinch from the poisonous venom of his tone. 'Unless you're trying to claim that he forced you?'

'I— He… No—I'm not claiming that…'

How could she do any such thing, even to save herself from this hellish embarrassment? She just wished that Dario would say something—anything—to break the tension that stretched tight between the three of them. But after that one demonic touch of humour, the coldly blazing scorn he had turned on her just moments before, he had now frozen where he stood, arms crossed over his broad chest, dark brows drawn together, a silent, watchful observer of the scene in front of him.

'Not that I'd put it past him,' Marcus stunned her by declaring now. 'A man with his reputation.'

'Rep...reputation?' Alyse managed, stunned to learn that Marcus seemed to know something about Dario—more, in fact, than she did herself. 'What...?'

But Marcus wasn't listening, intent instead on turning the venom he had directed at her previously onto Dario himself.

'Dragged up in the gutter by a mother who was anyone's for the price of—'

It was only the tiniest movement. Just a tensing of Dario's long body, a curl of his fists, a hint of a step forward. But that, when combined with the black thundercloud of his frown, the way his sensual mouth was clamped hard and tight into a thin line, was enough of a warning to have Marcus biting off the last of his insulting sentence and clearly backing down. He obviously didn't think that it was safe to risk baiting Dario any further, however much he might want to.

And the other man's reaction turned Alyse's legs to water at the memory of the way that this had been just what she had planned as part of her original scheme in the first place. It had all seemed so exciting, so brilliant—so *possible* when she had come up with the idea as a way of getting rid of Marcus's unwanted attentions. Give him the impression that she was involved with another man, that she was seeing someone else—maybe even sleeping with someone else—and then surely he would back off and leave her in peace?

But now, finding herself in exactly the situation she had anticipated, with Marcus at the door, having found her and Dario in a decidedly compromising situation—far more compromising than she had ever planned—things were not at all as she had foreseen. For one thing, Marcus, though looking disgusted and furious, didn't seem to have the intention of turning round and walking away, as he had in her mind when she'd imagined this happening.

And Dario...

She risked a glance at the tall, dark, glowering man to her left, and immediately wished she hadn't. He wasn't actually snarling but he might as well have been and she could practically see his hackles rising in hostile threat to the intruder into his territory. The sparks that seemed to flash between the two men made her feel like some tasty but already wounded prey that was the subject of a face to face confrontation between two powerful and equally ravenous lions.

Giving up on trying to fasten her dress, she folded her arms tightly around her waist, as much to hold herself together as to keep the blue silk from falling into a pool on the carpet at her feet.

'No matter what my reputation,' Dario drawled now, making Alyse start because she was so used to him being silent, 'it seems that Alyse doesn't give a damn about it, *mi caro fratello.*'

My—*what?* Alyse shook her head faintly, unable to believe she had heard right. The stress must be getting to her so that she was imagining things. He couldn't have said...

But, whatever he had said, it had been deliberately provocative. And it had the desired effect, enraging Marcus so that his whole face went white with fury, pulling taut over his bones.

'Marcus...' she tried, desperate to have this appalling stalemate broken, to avoid what she was now starting to fear might actually bring these two to blows. There was something here between these two that was evil. Something she didn't understand but if she could just avoid an actual fight...

'Look, I'm sorry if this has upset you, but really you know I never said...'

He wasn't listening, all his attention focused on Dario's hard, set face. But, even as she watched, Alyse was stunned to see the faint flicker of a smile on the Italian's sensual lips. A smile that was there and gone again in a moment and had nothing warm about it at all.

'I could kill you...'

Marcus's threat, directed at Dario's impassive face, was a low, savage mutter, one that sent a horrified shiver slithering down Alyse's spine. In a panic she stepped forward, her hand coming out as she forgot about holding her dress up and could only think about stopping him.

'Marcus, I tried to tell you that I couldn't see any future for us, so I thought—'

'Thought you'd teach me a lesson?'

'No—I...'

But her voice had no strength, no conviction. Wasn't that really what she had wanted to do? To convince him that she was not for him? That she wasn't at all interested in the proposal he had pushed at her so unexpectedly and had kept pushing for days.

'You thought you'd rub my face in it,' he snarled, the look he turned on her scraping over her body like the burn of acid.

It was only now, when that hateful look paused and lingered deliberately, that Alyse became aware of the betraying damp, darkened patches directly over her breasts where Dario's hot mouth had sought out the sensitive peaks that had strained against her bra. The realisation dried her throat in a moment.

'No...' she tried but, even though her lips moved, no sound managed to come out. And when she glanced uncertainly at Dario, the darkness and focus of his eyes told her that he had something else on his mind other than belief in her declaration.

From a shadowy corner of her thoughts came an uncomfortable memory of the time in the car when she had looked back and seen Marcus staring after them. She'd been careless enough to smile just briefly. And Dario had caught it. Could he think this was what she had wanted?

'Well, you couldn't have made a better job of it than this, you bitch.' Marcus was continuing his rant. 'You must have known if there was one thing that would guarantee I'd want nothing more to do with you—something that would turn my stomach—it was the sight of you getting down and dirty with my bastard brother.'

CHAPTER THREE

My bastard brother.

This time there could be no doubt about it, though Alyse's thoughts reeled in disbelief at what she heard. She hadn't been sure earlier—*mi caro fratello*—but in plain, straightforward English it couldn't be clearer.

But that just wasn't possible—was it? Marcus was a solid, stolid Englishman with the pale colouring and eyes that marked him out as pure Anglo-Saxon. He had nothing of Dario's stunning golden skin and sleek black hair. Those blue, blue eyes that met hers in a stare of blank confrontation were the only thing that could seem to connect the two. And *bastard* brother...

'Half-brother, to be more accurate,' Dario put in now, though it stuck in his throat to even acknowledge that connection. 'Though definitely the bastard.'

She hadn't known that—or certainly not all of it, he realised. If the confusion that was written on her pale face was genuine. Somehow she had managed to avoid hearing about the scandal that had exploded in the gossip columns years ago when he had turned up at the Kavanaugh home to carry out his mother's last wishes and claim acknowledgement from his family. But that was impossible, surely. When her father was employed by Marcus and his father, tangled up in everything the younger man did, then even Lady Alyse Gregory must know something of what was going on.

'I...'

That unsettled stare went from his face to Marcus's and back again, no sign of anything but confusion showing in it. So it hadn't been because of who he was that she had chosen him. Obviously any man would have done.

So would she have gone through with it if they hadn't been so rudely interrupted? Or had she calculated this down to the precise second so that they would be caught together at just the last possible moment?

'The last man whose leavings I'd want to touch.' Marcus was really feeling savage now.

Oh, that had hit home. He had caught her on the raw there, and Dario had to admit to a twist of admiration at the way her head came up, her eyes flashed. At last she looked like the woman she was. The product of years of aristocratic heritage, of pure blue-blooded breeding. The woman Henry Kavanaugh dreamed of having as the mother of his grandchildren.

'I'm nobody's leavings! And if you hadn't refused to take no for an answer, then I wouldn't have been forced to...'

The impetus given her by the rush of indignation had obviously ebbed, and she turned a wary, uncertain look on Dario, clearly realising that she had just dug herself even deeper into the hole she found herself in. There was more to that look too. She wasn't asking but summoning him to her aid. She actually expected him to come to her assistance, confirm her story. But if she thought he was going to give her a helping hand, then she had better think again. That 'forced' had hit home, barbs sticking into his skin.

'I wouldn't have had to...'

The careful amendment did nothing to soothe Dario's

mood. He was keeping out of this one until she had decided which way she was going to jump.

'You'll regret this.' Marcus's tone was low and savage.

'I already do.'

So now they were getting closer to the truth. That last
comment had the ring of conviction in it. Obviously Lady
Alyse Gregory would regret her unthinking and indiscreet
lapse of control. Particularly as she had now discovered
that she had thrown herself into the arms of the Italian
bastard that Marcus had revealed him to be.

Clearly his half-brother thought so too. There was actually a smile of triumph in those pale eyes.

'And nothing happened? Then come with me now and
we'll forget all about this foolishness.'

Wrong move, brother, Dario thought to himself. Even
on his short acquaintance with her, he was pretty damn
sure that Alyse would not respond well to that autocratic
'come with me now'. The only way he could have made
matters worse would have been by snapping his fingers
at her as if he was calling a dog to heel.

And Alyse Gregory was no obedient pet. That was plain
from the way her mouth tightened, and she shook back the
mane of golden hair.

'No.'

She had to say it, Alyse acknowledged inwardly. There
was no other option. Given a choice in the matter, she
would have walked out of here right now and never looked
back at either Dario or Marcus. She had no idea just what
these two brothers—*brothers!*—were up to but she had
no wish to get caught in the middle of whatever personal
war they were intent on fighting.

But leaving meant letting Marcus think that he had won.
And that was the last thing she wanted. Hadn't she set out
on this crazy venture in the first place as a way of making

sure that he left her alone? That he stopped plaguing her with expressions of how beneficial it would be for the two of them, blending the aristocratic blood of her line with the wealth and security that he could bring to the table. She had never been able to get him to accept her refusal, and if she left with him now then it would all be to do again.

'No,' she tried again when he looked unconvinced.

'Alyse…'

'The lady said no,' Dario drawled unexpectedly from behind her. 'You lose.'

You lose! If earlier she had felt like some vulnerable prey, now the sensation was much more like some tasty bone being fought over by two bad-tempered dogs.

What did he think she was? Some sort of trophy—just a notch on his bedpost? Not that they had got as far as the bed! Just let them get rid of Marcus and she would make him pay for that.

Dario moved past her, taking hold of the door and moving it to block Marcus's entrance.

'Goodnight, Marcus,' he said pointedly.

'I swear you'll regret this.' It was so different this time. The voice of darkness with threat threaded through every word. 'You'll…'

'Goodnight, Marcus.'

Dario pushed the door even closer to being shut, blocking out the sight of Marcus's enraged face. Alyse found that she was holding her breath, not knowing what she would do if he refused to leave. Would they have to call the police?

She could just imagine what her father's reaction would be if she was involved in some scandal that hit the newspapers, tonight of all nights. He had asked her—begged her—not to rile Kavanaugh, to keep the family name out of the gossip columns. It would just destroy her mother, who had recently retreated into one of her black depressions. That was why she had decided on the plan that was supposed to make Marcus reject the idea of marriage. A plan that now seemed to have had more effect than she could ever have dreamed of.

'Damn you to hell, Olivero!' Marcus flung one more violent outburst at the other man.

But then, to Alyse's relief, he finally turned and marched off down the corridor, swearing as he went.

'At last.'

Dario kicked the door shut behind him, his smile an expression of grim satisfaction as he turned back to Alyse.

'I think we've seen the back of him.'

'Mmm...'

Alyse was preoccupied with finally hitching her dress up so that it sat securely on her shoulders again, struggling to get her hands on the pull of the zip at her waist, to restore her appearance to normality.

'So where were we?'

She hadn't seen him come closer, prowling soft as a hunting cat, so she jumped violently when he touched her, warm and soft on her cheek.

'What?' Her head snapped up, her fumbling grip freezing on the tab of the zip.

His hand was on her hair, long fingers tangling in the fall of blonde, smoothing through the silky strands when she realised just what he meant and tensed up sharply.

'You think we— You can just take up from where you left off?'

'Why not?' He actually sounded genuinely puzzled. 'What's changed?'

'What's... You...'

The words spluttered to a halt inside her head, shock, disbelief and sheer blind fury warring to find the uppermost spot. Fury won. It was the memory of that casually triumphant '*You lose*' that did it.

'You dare to think that nothing's changed?' She flung the words at him, not liking the way that they simply rebounded off his hard, set bone structure.

'Dare?' he echoed dangerously. 'What's to dare about it? We both know why you came here—or we did until dear Marcus interrupted everything. But now he's gone...'

And so had the mood. From the heated sensuality, the primal hunger she had been feeling before, she was now swamped with bitter disappointment that was the result of his cold conviction that they would just take up from where they had been interrupted. He made no concessions to the way that the mood had been shattered by his *brother's* arrival. The way they had fought over her like dogs over a bone.

The struggle to deal with the let-down made her feel as limp as a balloon that had been pricked by a pin, all the air slowly seeping away. She wasn't prepared to investigate the bitter sting that might have been disappointment.

Dario had made her feel wonderful. His touch had aroused her, his kiss had enticed her. But most of all he had made her feel beautiful— and special. She had wanted him so badly and thought that he wanted her too. But that had been before she had become aware of just who he was. Before she had been caught in the middle of the private war that Dario and Marcus were waging between them. She didn't know what had started it, but it was blatantly obvious that they detested each other and that they would do anything at all to score points over one another. She had no intention of being used to make Dario Olivero feel that his half-brother had lost and he had *won.*

'I don't think so.'

She twisted away from him, biting down hard on her lower lip to hold back the small cry of pain as his fingers caught in her hair, tugging painfully at her scalp. Refusing to let him see that it had hurt her, she tossed back the tumbled mane and looked him straight in those blue eyes. How had she never seen how cold they could become? Had her infatuation blinded her so that she hadn't recognised how much they resembled Marcus's eyes? They might be a deeper, richer blue, but the way they froze over when he was angry was exactly the same.

'What the hell's going on?'

She caught Dario's dark frown and made herself face it defiantly.

'Haven't you got it yet?' she challenged, almost defeated by the swift narrowing of those blue eyes, focusing them like lasers on her face. She forced herself to go on before her nerve failed her completely. 'This wasn't anything real. Not at all. It was just a bit of fun.'

'Fun.'

The way the word was snatched in through his clenched teeth was like the hiss of a cobra just before it sprang forward to bite. So much so that Alyse actually took a hasty step backwards, away from attack.

An attack that didn't come. Instead, Dario had frozen into complete stillness before her, his powerful body seeming to be carved from stone.

'Do you usually use people for *fun*?'

'I didn't use...'

Her courage failed her in the burn of his glare. She hadn't used him—at least not in the way he'd meant. But when she'd started out on this plan, with that crazy idea in her head, of playing for attention from someone else, then wasn't that using?

And hadn't that plan been at the forefront of her mind

when she had first seen Dario, dark and dangerously devastating, on the opposite side of the room?

'So are you claiming that you just met me—fell head over heels and into my arms?'

Pretty much, Alyse acknowledged to herself. But she wasn't going to admit that. His head was already way too big to let him know the effect he had on her. Knowing that he believed he was the winner, and Marcus the loser, she had no desire to feed his ego any more.

'As if...' she said scornfully, not caring if that just deepened his conviction that she had been using him from the start.

Any thought of *using* had ceased to be the case from the moment that she had met him face to face. It had flown out of the window, along with her self-control and any sense of self-preservation. She had thought that he felt the same too. But how could this hard-faced, blank-eyed, icy-voiced male standing before her ever have been capable of the sort of passion that she had believed had gripped him just as it had her?

Was it possible that he had known who she was from the start? That even their 'introduction'—that dance!—had been carefully planned, calculated for the best possible effect? Remembering now, she could recall how his eyes had narrowed when she had given her name. He had known who she was—and obviously he knew of Marcus.

'I want to go home.'

As she spoke she was looking round the room, hunting for the clutch bag she had discarded so carelessly in the moment that Dario had taken her into his arms, the shoes she had kicked off as he lifted her from the ground, carrying her towards the settee. Before the ominous bang at the door had smashed into the heated, unthinking mood.

'I want to go home,' she repeated when there was no response. Had he not heard her or was he totally withdrawn behind that cold, set mask that had covered his face?

'OK.'

If she'd thought he might object—that he would have tried to persuade her not to go—then she couldn't have been more mistaken. Instead, he just shrugged and turned away from her.

'Fine.'

A harsh gesture, just the contemptuous flick of one bronzed hand, pointed her across the room, away from him.

'There's the door.'

That was it. But had she hoped for anything more? Had she wanted him to argue, to try to persuade her otherwise? She had to be all sorts of crazy if that was so.

Padding across the floor in her stockinged feet, she grabbed her bag, picked up her shoes. Just the thought of trying to cram her feet into them again tonight was almost too much to take. She hadn't actually worn them properly since she had got into Dario's car to come here.

Here. She didn't even know where *here* was. She'd been too intent on Dario to notice any landmarks they might have passed.

'But how will I...?'

He didn't let her finish the question, anticipating perfectly just what she was about to say.

'The concierge downstairs will call you a taxi. Charge it to my account.'

And that was it—over—done with. He had switched off from her so completely she might already be out of the room. He hadn't been able to get what he wanted from her; she wasn't in his bed, which was all that he had planned on, so now he couldn't wait to be rid of her.

'Is this how you usually treat your dates?'

The deep blue glance he turned on her was cold enough to freeze right through to her soul, shrivelling everything inside her. A long pause, and then he raised one hand, the index finger extended deliberately.

'One,' he drawled coolly, ticking off the point with his other hand, 'this was no *date*. Merely a chance encounter. And, two—you were never *mine*.'

He didn't add the 'thank God' that was clearly on the tip of his tongue, but he didn't need to. She could read it in the iciness of his eyes, the burn of dismissal that seared her from head to toe.

'Now, would you mind leaving? I have things to do.'

To drive home the point, he flipped open the case of the tablet computer that was lying on a nearby table and tapped the screen, his attention focused firmly on the appliance.

It was as if she was no longer there, and if she had any sense at all left then she'd make sure that that was in fact the case. Without another word, she hurried across the room. He didn't even spare her another glance as she pulled open the door and made her way out of it.

She'd had a narrow escape there, Alyse admitted to herself as the door swung to behind her. She'd seen the flash of something dangerous in Dario's eyes before he had turned away and she was glad to get out of the room unscathed. She could only hope that Marcus wasn't still hanging about somewhere. He'd been furious but, strangely, in this uncomfortable aftermath she didn't feel half as unnerved by his blustering fury as she was by the glacial stare Dario had turned on her.

Dario, *Marcus's half-brother*!

Her mind still reeled under the impact of that revelation. How, at a huge event, in an enormous room crammed with hundreds of people—had she been unfortunate enough to pick on the one person who could put her in a worse situation than the one she had been trying to avoid? What was that saying about being caught between a rock and a hard place? Her legs suddenly unsteady, Alyse almost missed her step on the stairs and had to grab at the bannister for support.

She had got away this time and, with luck, she had convinced Marcus that there was no point at all in coming after her with his unwanted attentions. But was that the end of it? Why was she plagued by such a cold, sneaking suspicion that there was more to come?

That she had simply jumped right out of the frying pan and into the fire.

CHAPTER FOUR

THE RING OF the doorbell was the last thing that Alyse had been expecting.

The last thing she wanted too, if the truth was told. She was waiting for her father to come home because her mother had been asking for him and was getting more anxious with each minute that ticked by. She wasn't expecting—or wanting—any other visitors at the house tonight.

Her first instinct was to ignore the summons. Her father would never use the doorbell because of course he had his own key. Rose and Lucy, her best friends, were away on a skiing holiday, one she should have been sharing with them. But she had decided that her mother needed her more, her illness so bad this time that Alyse had had no option but to take leave from her job at the art gallery to give the twenty-four-hour care the older woman needed.

Marcus, thank heaven, seemed to have got the message after the encounter in Dario's apartment. He had not appeared at the house for the past couple of days, when before he had been on the doorstep at every opportunity, it seemed. A situation that had been made all the worse by the fact that her mother's depression was worse than it had been for some time.

So at first she sat still, hoping that she couldn't be seen from the street. But the unexpected visitor was clearly not being put off by the lack of response, and if she wasn't careful that persistent ringing at the doorbell would disturb her mother and have her coming downstairs.

Alyse prayed it wasn't Marcus again, coming back for round two. Well, in that case, perhaps he would be put off rather than attracted, she reflected as she caught a glimpse of herself in an ornately framed mirror that hung on the wall as she crossed the hallway. The simple red skirt and cream T-shirt she wore was hardly the look of any man's sexual fantasies. But surely Marcus had got the message by now.

The ringing at the door got louder, more strident, as if someone had pressed their finger on the bell and left it there.

'Oh, all right—I'm coming.'

She pulled open the door then stared in horror at the strong, dark figure standing on the doorstep.

'You!'

Dario Olivero might be far more casually dressed than the elegant evening wear of two nights before, but in the worn leather jacket, navy T-shirt and tight blue jeans he was no less impressive than on the night of the ball. If anything, the casual clothes threw the carved beauty of his features into stronger relief, and the faint glow of the spring sun in the garden made his tanned skin look golden against the sleek raven's wing colour of his hair.

'Me.'

For a moment, he hadn't quite recognised her, Dario admitted to himself. When the door to her father's house had first opened, he had thought that she might be some sort of domestic staff. The polish and sophistication of the glamorous society beauty he had seen at the ball was missing, the elegant silk gown replaced by a casual skirt and loose-fitting top, her feet pushed into simple flat pumps that matched the red of her skirt. Her hair hung loose around her shoulders, soft waves that his fingers itched to touch, and, even without a trace of make-up, her skin had a fresh, natural glow that made her look years younger than the twenty-three he knew her to be.

He had spent the past couple of days telling himself to forget the woman who had thought she could use him to anger his hated half-brother. Faced with this other, very different Alyse, he knew without a doubt just why he hadn't succeeded. The woman at the ball had haunted his thoughts, tormented his nights with burning fantasies of the moments she had been underneath him on the settee, her legs splayed to accommodate him, her mouth hot on his. But he had told himself that he wanted nothing more to do with a woman who'd planned only to use him to make his brother burn with jealousy. *This* woman drove all such thoughts from his mind and left him with a knowledge that rocked his sense of sanity. The knowledge that this woman was one he would never be able to forget.

That she was the reason he was here now, instead of forgetting her for good, as he had vowed only two nights before.

But the forty-eight hours that had passed in between had changed so much. Two days before, he would have been satisfied with putting a spoke in his half-brother's plan to use marriage to Alsye to secure his father's favour. Since then he had learned so much more about what was going on. And the delivery of a most unexpected letter, the first and only letter he had ever received from his father, one that had followed him here all the way from Tuscany, had only added to the shifting shadows behind everything that was being played out on the surface.

The depth of his brother's scheming had been no surprise. His father's intervention had been totally unexpected. But now that he had actually met Alyse, he had recognised that she at least was unaware of the darker schemes in which she was being used. She was as much at the mercy of her own father as he had once been at his.

He had vowed never again to let Marcus's cold-blooded scheming succeed if it was in his power to stop it. There was a much older vow too, one that he had made to his mother years before, a promise she had drawn from him on her deathbed. A vow that meant he had to respond to the slightest hint of reconciliation with his biological father, even if it stuck in his throat to do it.

And if that vow gave him more reason to see the beautiful Alyse Gregory—to get her into his life on his terms— then so much the better.

'What are you doing here?' The way that Alyse's heart had lurched against her ribs at the sight of him made the words come out breathless and uneven.

Dario smiled; at least that was what she thought his expression was meant to be. Just a grim twist of his mouth, the sensual lips curling up slightly at the corners.

'And hello to you too. Thank you for the welcome.'

'You're not welcome!'

If she had opened the door to find a waiting panther, sleek, black, dangerous, standing before her, her nerves couldn't have twisted any tighter into painful knots. And she couldn't get her heart rate to settle down into its normal steady beat.

'Fine.'

He was turning away, about to head off down the drive again to where a powerful car waited in the sunshine. It should have made her feel thankful, but instead the knots in her stomach tightened brutally and she was left with an uncomfortable nagging feeling that she had missed something.

After all, he had to have come here for some reason and she didn't trust his apparently easy response to her dismissal.

'Wait!'

At first she thought that he hadn't heard her or that if he had he wasn't going to respond. But then his long strides slowed, he came to a halt, turned a sidelong glance over his shoulder in her direction. And waited.

'Why have you come here?'

'I wanted to return something to you.'

'Return what?'

He turned at last, but slowly, almost lazily.

'Do you want to do this out here?'

'I suppose you'd better come in.'

She pushed the door wide and marched into the hall, leaving him to follow or not as he chose. He prowled after her and it was unnerving how she was aware of every step, every movement even though he was behind her. The whole atmosphere inside the house changed in a moment.

Had he brought the warmth of the garden inside with him? Or was it possible that just the heat of his body could alter the temperature so much? Because suddenly she felt uncomfortable in the long-sleeved shirt that only moments before had seemed perfectly fine for the day. The slam of the door as it closed behind Dario made her start so violently she was sure her feet had actually lifted several inches off the floor.

'OK.' She made herself swing round to face him. 'Just what is it you're returning to me?'

Dario's mouth quirked slightly in disconcerting amusement at her tone.

'A cup of coffee would be nice.'

'There's an Italian coffee bar down the street,' Alyse tossed at him, wanting this over and done with and him on his way.

He didn't take the bait but his eyes went to the partly open kitchen door through which, much to Alyse's fury, it was easy to see the coffee maker she had just filled and switched on before his knock had come at the door. The wonderful aroma of freshly brewed coffee filled the air.

'One coffee!' she conceded irritably.

She pushed open another door, the one that led into the sitting room, wanting him to go that way and so take away some of the pressure she felt. He wasn't even standing *close* to her, for heaven's sake! But Dario Olivero could fill a room simply by being in it, and the warm scent of his skin, the blue gleam of his eyes made her nerves burn in a heated response that she knew must show in the rise of colour to her cheeks.

'One coffee,' she muttered again, not really knowing whether she was trying to drive the point home to him or convince herself.

If it was Dario she was aiming her words at then they had no effect. When she made her way into the kitchen he was right behind her, silent-footed like a hunting tiger.

She opened a cupboard door, snatched two mugs from the shelves, banged them down on the worktop then reached for the glass jug of coffee. It shook in her hand, threatening to spill scalding coffee all over the surface, and it was the last straw for Alyse. Dumping it down on its hotplate, she swung round to face him, her breath snagging in her throat as she realised just how close he had come. She wanted to put out her hands, flatten them against the broad stretch of his chest under the clinging navy cotton and push him away. But, not knowing whether she would react too strongly, risking near violence in her response, or if the temptation to touch those corded muscles, feel the heat of his skin through the soft material might just be too much for her, instead she put her hands behind her, gripping tight to the edge of the worktop in order to stop them going anywhere more dangerous.

'So what is it that you say you want to return to me?' She emphasised that 'say' so that he could be in no doubt at all that she really didn't believe him.

'This.'

He reached into his jacket pocket, then held his hand towards her, palm upwards so that she could see something small and golden, the rich sheen of pearl gleaming against his skin.

'My earring!'

The earring she had worn on the night of the ball and had only realised that she had mislaid somewhere when she had undressed for bed, her still-shaking fingers only finding one piece of jewellery in her left ear lobe.

'I must have left it…'

'In my apartment.'

The quiet confirmation had no trace of triumph in it but, all the same, she felt as if the easy words had scoured a much needed protective layer from her skin. She couldn't meet his eyes, focusing all her attention on the earring in his hand, feeling really rather foolish. She had believed that it was all just a made-up story. She'd even allowed herself to think, just for a moment, that perhaps he hadn't been able to forget her. That he had actually wanted her far more than he had let on. That he might want more than just a heated one-night stand.

Instead, it was something much more ordinary, and he really was returning the piece of jewellery that he must have found after she had left. He would have done the same for anyone at all. It was nothing at all to do with *her*.

'Well...'

He was waiting for her to move, watching her intently, a gleam of something—amusement?—challenge?—in those blue eyes. His hand was still between them, palm held out, the earring nestling against the bronzed skin, and she knew that he was waiting for her to make a move to take it.

It would mean touching him. It would mean brushing the skin of his palm with her fingers, feeling its warmth, absorbing some trace of him...

When his mouth quirked at the corners again she knew that there was a definite challenge there. She had to move now or face the accusation of cowardice that was clearly hovering just at the tip of his tongue.

'Thank you.'

Swallowing down the twist of nerves, she reached forward, aiming to snatch it up without actually touching him. But the painful awareness of the way he was watching her meant that she mistimed the movement, fumbled clumsily, missed the earring and let it drop back onto his palm.

'Sorry...'

Dario bit down hard on his lower lip, catching back the unexpected laughter that almost escaped him. Alyse had struggled so hard not to let her fingers make contact with his in a vain pretence that she wasn't interested in him at all.

Who was she trying to fool? She had felt the phosphoric flare of response between them from the first moment and it was still there, no matter how hard she was trying to deny it. It was there, in her eyes, the wash of colour over those beautiful cheekbones, in the dryness of the lips she held partly open, breathing rather too fast, unevenly through the narrow space. If he had any doubt—which he did not—then it would all have been driven away by the fast, flurried slick of her tongue over the softness of her bottom lip, leaving behind a sheen of soft moisture on the unpainted skin.

The purely male urge to bend and take her mouth, tasting that essence of her, was almost uncontrollable. But, with a grim struggle, he forced it back down again fast, praying that she wouldn't see the fight he had to control his stinging arousal. If he so much as touched his mouth to hers it would not be enough. One taste, one brief moment of inhaling the special scent that was all her, and he would be lost. He would have to take more. And more. Until he buried himself in her body and was lost for good.

There was too much at stake to rush things now. He wanted this woman until his whole body hurt with need, but that wasn't the only reason why he had come here today. This was no everyday seduction. She was the key to beating his half-brother once and for all; and maybe even to opening the door into his father's world just a tiny crack.

Because, for once, it seemed that Marcus, uncharacteristically, had played his hand close to his chest, and when he had seen Alyse face up to his brother he had known that she was the person to have on his side in this.

'Your earring,' he said pointedly, unable to suppress a smile as she still hesitated, her fingers hovering just above the tiny item of jewellery where it rested on his palm.

But then she clearly gathered herself. Those green eyes flashed upwards, just once, at his face. Part defiance, part challenge of her own that made him want to meet her head-on, take what he wanted right now and not have to bide his time, to watch and plan.

He'd never had to wait for a woman before. But this time, with her, he reckoned she'd be worth it.

So he tilted his hand slightly towards her, angling it, encouraging...

'Ms Gregory.'

'Thank you.'

Her tone might have been stiff and formal but her touch was not. It was fast and awkward, snatching at the pearl in a way that made his skin burn where she touched him. The faint scrape of the pale pink painted nails against his skin made a burn of hungry heat pool low in his body. It was all he could do not to curl his fingers up, closing over hers, to hold her, draw her closer to him.

But not yet. She was already as wary as a wild bird he had enticed to come closer by laying down a trail of breadcrumbs. Move too fast and she would fly away.

'You're welcome,' he told her, smiling inwardly as he saw the way her shoulders relaxed at the careful formality of his tone. 'So—about that coffee? Black, no sugar.'

'Of course...'

Coffee was the last thing he wanted, but he could enjoy taking the opportunity to watch her as she went about making it, the press of her neat bottom against the red cotton of her skirt, the elegant length of her legs as she stood on tiptoe, reaching up to collect the milk from a shelf in the fridge. His fingers itched to stroke her silky hair and he rammed them hard into the pockets of his jeans to keep them away from temptation.

'Heard anything from Marcus lately?'

The question was almost Alyse's undoing and she had to bang the milk bottle down onto the glass shelf in a pretence that she was responding to his comment that he didn't want it. She'd been glad to turn her back on him, needing to get away from the sensual pull he exerted simply by existing. She'd thought she'd managed to control herself pretty well, welcoming the chance to turn away before she betrayed herself, but now he was threatening her composure in a very different way with the unexpected question.

'No—nothing.'

Concentrating fiercely on pouring coffee into mugs, she was still aware of some inexplicable tension in his lean body, one that had been echoed in the apparently innocuous question.

'But then why would I? He must have got the message on Monday night.'

If his question had been unnerving, then his silence now was even more disturbing. Mug in one hand, she swung round to face him.

'You don't think he got the message?'

It hit hard to think that she might not be free of Marcus as she had hoped. After two months of persistent pressure, she had been so looking forward to getting her life back on track. All she'd needed was for her mother to feel well again. Or so she'd thought.

'Oh, I've no doubt he saw just what you were trying to tell him. But if you think that will be an end to it then you're very much mistaken. It's not the message he wants and I've never known my brother to give up on anything he wants if he's determined it's for him.'

'And he's determined that—what is for him?'

Dario reached forward, took the mug from her precarious hold but made no attempt to drink from it.

'You, of course.'

'What?'

He was joking. He had to be joking; he couldn't possibly be serious. But his eyes had no amusement glinting in them, and there wasn't even the hint of a smile around that sexy mouth.

No—that was a mistake. Looking directly at his mouth threatened to drive away the ability to think, to follow through the questions that his reply had stirred in her mind. And she had to think; his sombre expression told her that. It also warned that there was more to this than she had ever anticipated. But all she could think of was the feel of that mouth on hers, the taste of it, the hard pressure… and then its heated caress over her skin, down her neck…

'But I—on Monday, I—we—made him think…'

'Don't imagine that that will put Marcus off for good.'

'He can't want *me* that much. Oh, OK, he has been showing me attention for a while—but it's only just lately that he has become more insistent.'

Just before her mother had become ill again this time. Ellen Gregory had had one of her manic moods just after Christmas and she had been high on life, enjoying herself, she'd said, going out to events, to parties where neither Alyse nor her husband had been able to go with her. Then, three weeks ago, she had fallen down into the expected slump, retreating to her bedroom and not talking to anyone. Alyse had seen the change in her father's demeanour then too; he had become quiet and withdrawn as well.

It had been around that time that Marcus had started calling round even more regularly. It was also when her father had asked her to encourage him—or at least not to reject him out of hand. She didn't understand just why Antony Gregory had suddenly become Marcus's advocate but she'd tried. After all, he was the son of her father's boss and she didn't want to cause any trouble between them.

But Marcus had become just too insistent. He'd been dropping hints about the possible repercussions if she turned him down. That was when she had come up with the plan for the night of the ball. She had been sure that if he saw her with someone else—someone she seemed so much keener on than him—then he would get the message and back off. In fact, the only good part of that whole humiliating evening was the thought that at least Marcus would stay away. But now Dario was claiming that his half-brother would not be deterred by anything that had happened.

'No...' She shook her head worriedly, struggling all over again with that feeling of being a bone being fought over by two determined dogs.

'Yes...'

Dario put down his untouched coffee mug on the nearest worktop and reached for her. Still so disorientated by the unexpected news, she let him lead her out into the hall, where he turned her until she was facing the long, ornately framed mirror in which she had glimpsed herself earlier as she'd crossed the hall.

'Look at yourself...'

It was murmured against her hair, the warmth of his breath brushing over the soft skin of her neck. Momentarily, her eyes closed as she fought against the need to lean back into his warmth, to feel the strong support of his body, let the scent of his skin enclose her. But immediately they snapped open again as she recognised the danger of giving in to the temptation.

'Plain, pale and unsophisticated,' she returned tartly, green eyes clashing with his blue ones in the reflection in the mirror.

His mouth was partly hidden but she felt his laughter in the length of his body rather than seeing his smile.

'And you expect me to believe that? So tell me, Alyse, are you fishing for compliments?'

One bronzed hand stroked the blonde hair back from one side of her face, tucking it behind her left ear, and the feel of his touch made her shiver in needy response. A pulse that throbbed through her body centred between her legs, making her ache in yearning.

'Because I'll feed you flattery every minute of the hour, if that's what you want. Is that how Marcus wooed you, hmm? Was it by praising your beauty, telling you he had fallen head over heels for you?'

Something like that, Alyse acknowledged inwardly. He had told her she was beautiful—told her that he wanted her. But that had been at the very beginning. Just lately he had been pushing for marriage without any care or compliments. He'd insisted she would never find anyone better than him. That it would be to her advantage to accept his proposal.

But the scary thing was that where Marcus's compliments had sounded excessive, insincere, disturbingly so, she wanted to trust Dario—to believe that the words he described as flattery were real.

'Is that what you want? Will that please you?' he asked now, and something in his tone snapped her out of the foolish, hypnotic daydream that she had been lulled into.

'Not when you don't mean it!'

Snatching her head away from his caressing hands, she whirled round to face him so fast that her hair swung out around her head, slapping him in the face and catching on his eyelashes, the hint of late-in-the-day stubble at his jaw, trailing across his mouth.

Slowly he reached up, brushed it away carefully, fingers lingering on the soft strands.

'Just what is happening?' she demanded. 'Why did you really come round here this afternoon?'

She knew she wasn't going to get any answer she wanted when his face remained cold and unyielding, the muscles around his mouth tightening, drawing it into a thin line.

'Ask your father,' he tossed at her, cold and hard.

'What does my father have to do with this? I'm asking you. What is this between you and your brother— half-brother,' she amended hastily when she saw the flare of rejection in his eyes.

'That is none of your business.'

'But you're making it mine—you and Marcus are bring-ing it to my door, and I don't want it. I don't want to get caught up in your nasty, petty little civil war... What?'

Her nerves skittered, making her heart jolt against her ribs as she saw the way he shook his head, his mouth grim.

'I'm afraid you can't say that. You're already involved—and it isn't just you.'

Cold sensations slithered down her spine at his words. Her throat felt blocked, as if there was something tight-ening round it, making it impossible to breathe naturally. Sucking in a deep, much-needed gasp of air, she forced words from lips that were suddenly painfully dry.

'You've danced around this for too long, Dario—and I've had enough! I want you to tell me just what you mean. You claim that you and your brother are involved and who else?'

'All of you,' Dario put in when she struggled to go on. 'You—your father—your mother...'

'My mother?'

Now she was worried. The thought of her mother, shut in her room upstairs, the curtains drawn to block out the sunlight, the bedclothes pulled over her head as she fought the demons of her depression, twisted in the pit of her stomach. She knew that Ellen had been high—higher than usual—for some weeks so that the moment when she came tumbling down must inevitably feel truly low in contrast—but was there something more than that? Something that threatened even more darkness.

'What do you mean? Stop throwing out veiled threats...'

'Not threats, Alyse—at least not from me. Marcus is the one who is threatening you and your family. He is the one who holds your future in his hands—or thinks he does.'

She wanted to scream, to turn her hands into fists and

pummel them against his chest—anything to stop him
playing with her as a hunting cat toyed with a mouse. But
instead she fought to gather her composure.

'Tell me.'

Dario pushed both hands through the thickness of his
hair. His eyes searched her face, seeming to be looking for
evidence that she really wanted to know the truth. What he
saw must have convinced him because he gave a faint nod.

'Your mother has been gambling—at the casino.'

'That's not possible...' Alyse put in. Her mother had
been so depressed recently. 'She hasn't been out of the
house for days—a couple of weeks.'

Instinctively, her head turned towards the staircase,
listening for any sound that might indicate her mother
had actually emerged. But all was silent, as it had been
all afternoon.

'This was a couple of months back.'

When Ellen had been in a hyper state, full of zest and
the conviction that nothing could go wrong with her life.
Alyse fought to control a shiver at the dreadful possibili-
ties. In one of her high phases, her mother had no sense
of restraint or of danger.

'How much did she lose?'

The amount he named made her head spin, turned her
knees to water. And the black cloud that had been hovering on the horizon came rushing closer with a terrible
sense of inevitability.

'There's no way we can afford to pay that amount off—
not all in one go.' Or even if they were allowed to pay by
instalments; it would still be ruinous.

Something in Dario's face told her that this was not all
of it. There was more—and obviously worse—to come.

'Go on. Exactly what has Marcus to do with this?'

'He really hasn't told you?' His laughter was a sound

of incredulity, the humour grim, as dark as could be, and
he shook his head in disbelief as he spoke. 'You surprise
me—he has been so much more subtle than I'd ever anticipated. Or perhaps he's learned how to play the clever
game—close to his chest after all.'

'He...'

From the back of her mind slid a memory of the day
before the ball. Marcus had started to say something...
'Your father wants this every bit as much as I do. More.'
And later, her father—her father who had looked so pale
and strained recently, but she had put that down to concern about her mother—

'My father...' The strength had gone from her voice,
leaving it just a whisper. Her father had encouraged her
to see Marcus, to welcome him to the house. Then he had
encouraged her none too subtly to consider the younger
man's proposal.

But it was worse than she could ever have imagined.
Her father had tried to help his wife by taking the money
she needed secretly from the company he worked for.

'Embezzlement...' It was a horrible word. A scary word.

Even scarier if you stopped to think just who her father
had taken the money from.

'Kavanaughs... Oh, Dad, how could you?'

Alyse knew that the colour had leached from her face.
She could feel it seeping away as her heart slowed in horror.

So now she knew just why her father had looked so low,
so worn for the past few weeks. He had tried to save her
mother and only got in deeper as a result. Then he hadn't
actually pushed her towards marriage with Marcus, but he
had made it plain that he would be glad if it was to happen. Of course he would. The Kavanaughs would be unlikely to sue the man who was to be Marcus's father-in-law.

'No wonder he wanted me to agree to marry Marcus.'

But it still didn't explain why Marcus had suddenly become so determined on pushing for *marriage*. Pushing so hard, making her feel so trapped, that in the end she had determined on the crazy plan to get away from his attentions. Not knowing the full truth behind everything, she had taken a wild, thoughtless leap.

I swear you'll regret this. Marcus's words, ominously threatening, came back to haunt her. She had thought she'd got away with avoiding the issue of his proposal, but she had never known the darker elements behind it. The threat that Marcus could now hold over her. It was as if the sun had gone right behind a thick bank of cloud, leaving her shivering in miserable shock.

'You knew all this?'

'I do now.'

He'd known about Marcus's original reasons for wanting to marry Alyse, of course, Dario acknowledged privately. The way that his half-brother had set out to win his father's approval by fulfilling the older man's dream of linking the Kavanaugh family with the Gregorys. An aristocratic daughter-in-law and then, hopefully, later a titled grandson. It would be the final way of achieving a long-held ambition that Henry had failed to achieve for himself.

But not this. He'd known his half-brother was a louse and always had been. But he'd never anticipated finding out about this particularly vicious piece of blackmail. And they called *him* the bastard son!

'But you didn't think to tell me the other night?'

'I didn't know it all then and, for all I knew, you might have been totally happy to marry Marcus. It wasn't until I saw you with him that I realised you weren't that keen.'

'So you decided to have me all to yourself!'

A lazily raised eyebrow quirked in response to her outburst. 'While you were busy using me to get rid of my half-brother.'

'After you'd used me to make him angry—jealous.'

He wasn't going to deny that. It had been his plan at first. He'd seen an opportunity to thwart Marcus and had taken it. One small taste of payback for all the years of viciousness from the man who society called his brother. But now it seemed that Fate had handed him a stronger case for a true revenge—and maybe even a way to make his father notice him at last.

And a way to get this woman into his bed until this sexual hunger that flared like phosphorus between them burned itself out. He would make it worth her while, and it would certainly be to his advantage in every way.

'I reckon we both used each other.'

His casual shrug was bad enough, Alyse thought, but the smile that went with it was appalling. Like his carelessness, it was cold, callous, unfeeling. It told her that she had meant nothing to him—except as a weapon to use against his brother.

'Well, I hope you enjoyed yourself!' A heavy strand of hair fell forward over her face as she flung the words at him, and she reached up a hand to push it back. 'Was it fun? Satisfying?'

'Not as satisfying as I'd hoped...' Dario began but then she saw his mood change abruptly as his eyes followed the movement of her hand and his frown alerted her to the fact that something was wrong. 'Alyse...'

'What...?' Alyse managed as he reached forward fast, caught her hand, turned it towards her. 'Oh...'

The pearl earring, forgotten all this time, slipped from her hand to land on the tiled floor with a small clatter. But Alyse wasn't watching where it fell. She was staring at her hand, at the imprint of the jewellery where the earring had been clenched tightly in her grip. So tightly that it had dug into her palm, breaking the skin and making it bleed.

'Oh!'

'Here—let me...'

He had her hand in his, smoothing her fingers out of the way as he pulled a handkerchief from his pocket, wiped it softly over the torn skin. Then he rolled the cloth into a pad and pressed it down on the small wound, curling her fingers over it to hold it in place. His touch was warm and surprisingly gentle.

She'd hardly lost any blood but still her head swam and she felt faint. His dark head was bent over her hand, the scent of his hair and his skin reaching up like an intoxicating cloud to stir her senses even more. If she just made the tiniest movement then her hand would brush against its softness, making her want to clench her fingers tight around it, hold him closer. Surely, this near to her, he must hear the heavy pounding of her heart, see the throb of her pulse, blue under the skin at her wrist.

'Dario...'

It was just a whisper, thick with the reaction of her senses to his strength, but this time a strength used to help rather than to restrain or to hurt.

'Alyse...' His own response brushed his mouth against the place where her pulse beat, the warm stroke of his lips making her legs weaken, her whole body swaying towards him. It was still there, hot and strong, no matter how hard she might fight against it; she was still lost at the feel of his touch, the caress of his lips. She wanted to reach out and smooth her free hand down his cheek, know the warmth of his skin, the faint roughness of the bristle that shadowed his jawline.

She wanted more...

'Alyse...!'

It was her name again but called in a very different voice, in a very different way. High-pitched and sharp and slightly petulant, it came from the higher floor of the house, floating down the stairs to where they stood in the hall.

'Alyse!'

'Mum…'

She turned to head for the stairs, found his hand had closed over hers and she had to pull against it but he wouldn't free her. When she swung back to face him he was looking deep into her face, the smoky darkness of his eyes telling their story of hungry desire, so like the sting-ing need his kiss had woken inside her. Whatever this was, it had reached out and ensnared them both so that it only needed the tiniest connection to start it all off again.

'I have to go!' It was an angry whisper, even though she knew that her mother's bedroom was too far away for her to be heard. 'My mother needs me. She *needs* me!' she added more forcefully when his dark head moved in stark denial of her reaction.

'Don't go…'

Did he know what it did to her to hear that softly husky voice, the mixture of command and entreaty that threat-ened to tie her insides into knots as her own need warred with the sense of duty—and despair—that her mother's call had woken in her?

'I have to see what she needs. I *have* to…' she repeated when his grip on her hand had loosened and it was some-thing much more basic and primitive that kept her from moving. 'I have to do something! After all, there's noth-ing I can do about everything else.'

If she looked for an answer in his face, then there wasn't one there. His eyes were closed off from her, just blue opaque ice, revealing no feeling at all. He'd presented her with the details of Marcus's plan—marry him or see her father go to jail—and now it seemed he was prepared to leave her right in the lion's den.

'I have no defence against Marcus. There's nothing to fight with.'

He blinked just once, drew in a breath that seemed to go right to his soul.

'There is,' he said, his voice rough and husky. 'There's me.'

Alyse's eyes wouldn't focus. She couldn't see what was in his face, didn't know how to interpret it. He couldn't mean…could he? But if he meant what he said, then what else was involved in it? She longed to reach out and meet him halfway, and yet she didn't know what he was offering so the thought of it terrified her in the same seconds that she wanted it so much. Because, whatever he offered, she knew it had to come at a price.

Men like Dario didn't offer help—particularly not help to the extent that would be needed to solve this terrifying dilemma—without wanting something out of it for themselves.

She didn't know how to answer him, and her mind felt as if it was being torn in two. So it was a relief to hear her mother's voice calling to her again, that sharp-toned 'Alyse!' more demanding now, more urgent. Grateful for this one thing that she *had* to focus on, she tore her hand from Dario's, forced her feet into motion, ran up the stairs two at a time until she reached the half landing part way up.

Gasping for breath in a way that had nothing to do with her fitness or the steepness of the stairs, she came to a sudden halt, leaned over the bannister, looked down into the hall and into his face, upturned to watch her. He hadn't moved an inch but was standing exactly where she had left him, obviously waiting for an answer, knowing she would have to give him one.

'Wh-what...?' she stammered, fighting to get the words past the knot in her throat, the uneven beat of her heart. 'How...?'

The curl of his mouth told her that he had been expecting her reaction. She needed him and she had no one else to turn to. And he had only had to wait for her to realise that.

'Tomorrow,' he said quietly, almost casually. 'I'll give you till tomorrow. Come to me then and I'll tell you everything.'

And with another of those half-smiles, cool, careless and touched with a deep, dark satisfaction, he turned on his heel and strolled out of the door.

CHAPTER FIVE

'YOU CAN'T MEAN IT!'

Alyse's glass froze halfway to her mouth, then was set down again with a distinct crash as it landed on the polished wood of the dining table.

'I don't believe it! You have to be joking.'

'No joke.'

Dario toyed with the base of his own wineglass, his attention seeming to be elsewhere, though that was something that Alyse knew to be a pretence. He might not be giving her the focused attention she was directing at him but he was fiercely aware of how she was reacting. He knew her gaze was directed straight at him, he just didn't choose to meet it or show any response. He'd made the blunt, emotionless announcement and now he was waiting for her to calm down before he discussed further details.

But how could she calm down when what he had suggested was *this*?

'I said that I would help you and I will—but on my terms.'

And it was those terms that had made her head swim.

'I don't understand—why do we have to get married?'

'You make it sound as if it was a sentence of execution.'

It might almost be the same, Alyse admitted to herself. Except that at least a summary execution would be short, fast and over with.

'It's a lifetime's sentence.'

'Really?'

The look he turned on her now was sceptical and frankly questioning.

'I offered marriage—not commitment and devotion for life.'

Well, that told her, didn't it? If she had been dreaming of rings and flowers and happy ever afters then that fantasy had just been splattered in the dust at her feet. But then she hadn't been dreaming at all, except of a chance of a way out of the terrible situation she now found herself in. The truth was that she was still so stunned at the thought that he had actually said that he would help that she'd had no possible idea just what Dario might be prepared to do.

She'd been an idiot, she realised now. No one was going to offer to help her and her family pay the huge debts that had mounted up without demanding something pretty steep in return.

But this!

'Doesn't marriage usually demand both of those—or at least the intention of both of them?'

'If you believe that then you must have stars in your eyes. Oh, perhaps some idealistic fools set out with the idea of keeping those vows they make, but they very rarely stick to it. At least we'll know where we stand—a marriage of convenience to get us both what we want.'

'Just a marriage of convenience.'

She struggled to match him for calmness and certainty but it was impossible. She might not have been dreaming of rings and flowers and happy ever afters with this man—she'd have been crazy to contemplate it—but deep down she flinched away from the description of marriage that he'd put before her. One day, some day, she had hoped that she would meet someone who would love her as her father loved her mother, above and beyond everyone else. Surely every woman dreamed of having a man feel that way about her?

'One with a planned ending,' Dario continued. 'So there are no mistakes, no illusions. No one can claim they were led into it blindfolded.'

'Of course not.'

The smooth stretch of polished wood between them on the table suddenly seemed like a huge expanse of arid desert. The meal he had served her lay congealing on her plate, impossible to eat.

'I certainly couldn't claim that.'

In fact, when he had first made the suggestion it had been so blunt that she hadn't been able to believe she had heard right. So much so that her initial response had been to demand, 'Is this meant to be a proposal? Because it really doesn't sound like it.'

'You didn't exactly sugar-coat it.'

'I don't usually soft-pedal on my business deals,' Dario retorted.

Well, she knew that. She might only have had a few hours since he had left the house and before she obeyed his summons to come round to his apartment, but she'd put them to good use. She'd spent an age on the internet, finding out all she could about Dario Olivero—and there was a lot to find out. His origins might have been hazy, and it was obvious that he had grown up in circumstances very different from the power and affluence he knew now. In fact, it seemed that he had had no connection with the Kavanaugh family or their wealth until just a year or so before. Which explained why she had never heard of him, even though her family had known Marcus's for years.

But where his beginnings were shadowy and dark, he had soon left that part of his life behind. He had built himself the hugely successful wine business in Tuscany, winning award after award for the full-bodied reds, the subtle whites his vineyards produced. No doubt he had provided wines for the Kavanaughs' hotels and that was how he had come into contact with his half-brother. He had certainly built an empire to match—and outstrip—theirs, which was why he could now offer to take on her mother's debts and remove the threat of arrest and prosecution for her father. He had made a fortune several times over because of exactly what he had just said—that he was known for ruthlessness and determination in all his business dealings as in the rest of his life.

Oh, yes, the ruthlessness extended to his relationships too, apparently. No woman stayed around too long—though there had been plenty of them, all beautiful, wealthy and glamorous. But their regular turnover was proof, if she needed proof, of the fact that he had meant that declaration that he wasn't offering 'commitment and devotion for life'.

But exactly what was he offering—and why?

'I checked everything you said with my father,' she said, playing for time.

'I knew you would.'

'He confirmed everything.'

'I knew he would.'

It had to have been the most uncomfortable and upsetting conversation she had ever had with her father. Antony Gregory had blustered at first, then broken down, and in the end she could see that he had been barely holding on to his self-control and his eyes had been swimming with tears. Alyse had been appalled to see how low he had sunk. Even at this late stage, she had let herself hope it might not be as bad as Dario had revealed. Instead, she had found that it was already so much worse. Her father's embezzlement of funds from the Kavanaugh business had been discovered; Marcus had threatened him with exposure, with arrest... And she could be in no doubt at all that her own behaviour on the night of the ball had made things so much worse.

'Marcus is clearly out for revenge for what he saw as his huge humiliation, and he told Dad that he has just until the end of the week to "sort something out" before the police are informed...'

The memory of her father's face floated before her. But those tears had been for his wife—and himself—not for his daughter or the way he had been pushing her into a marriage that she loathed the thought of. In the past twenty-four hours so much had been turned on its head. With the realisation of just how both her parents had been involved in putting her neck in the noose that now surrounded it, she was forced to look again at the image of marriage they presented.

She could still have no doubt that her father loved his wife. So much that he would risk his own name, his freedom, in order to protect the woman he adored. There were those who would say that Antony Gregory loved not wisely but too well, and Alyse had once felt that way, too. But the revelations of the past days had rocked her world, shattering everything she had once had confidence in. Everything she'd thought she knew—the financial security of her home, her faith in her parents—had been snatched away from her, and she was left knowing she had been lied to, used as a pawn by the people she should have been able to trust the most.

'Which is why you're here.'

Could anything make him show any sort of emotion?

All through the meal he had remained sphinx-like, almost unmoving. He had eaten as little as she had, though Alyse couldn't possibly imagine that he was as nervous and apprehensive as she was, but that he must be as sparing in his appetite for food as he was in his movements and the stark elegance of his clothes. An immaculate white linen shirt hugged the powerful lines of his shoulders and exposed the bronzed skin of his throat where it was open at the neck. Black trousers hugged the lean hips and long legs, his narrow waist emphasised by the leather belt with a heavy silver buckle.

Obviously he hadn't had the crisis of confidence that had assailed her as she'd prepared for this evening. After the talk with her father she had had no doubt just how important this meeting was but as she didn't know just what to anticipate, it had been difficult to work out exactly what to wear.

In the end, deciding this was, after all, a business meeting, she had picked out a pale green shift dress that was one of the ones she wore to work, adding metallic flats and pulling her hair back into a high ponytail. It had seemed right at the time—but now…

What the heck did you wear to a businesslike proposal of marriage?

'I appreciate so much that you're offering to help…but… but why do we have to be married?' Her voice trembled so much that it mangled the last word.

'Can you think of anything else that would really put Marcus off? Because, believe me, if we're to deal with this problem properly, it won't just be possible to offer to pay off your father's debts and be done with it.'

'It won't?'

Was there something else behind all this—something he wasn't telling her? But he had said 'we' and she had to hold on to that. She couldn't do this alone and she was relieved and strengthened to think of having Dario's ruthless determination on her side. He, at least, was offering her a way out.

'Why not? Surely an engagement...'

Dario put down his glass and studied her across the width of the table. The candles flickered in a faint draught, throwing different, changing patterns over her pale face, shadowing her eyes. The sky beyond the windows was darker than he had realised, bringing home to him the fact that the evening was closing in around them. She had arrived later than he had anticipated, obviously because she had taken the time to have the much-needed talk with her father. But time was not what they had much of—not if they were going to make sure that Marcus didn't get the upper hand.

'An engagement won't be enough.'

An engagement might deter his half-brother but it would never fulfil the demands their father had made; the conditions he had put into his newly changed will.

Dario's grip tightened on the stem of his glass until the knuckles showed white. It had come as one hell of a shock to realise how ill his father had been over the past months. So much so that he had changed his will—and had actually written to his illegitimate son to let him know about it.

Coming that close to death, Henry Kavanaugh had feared that his long-held dream to have a grandchild, preferably one with a claim to a title, would never be realised. He held no illusions about Marcus and his louche lifestyle, so he had made marriage the condition for a very special bequest in his will. Being a cunning old fox, he had decided to hedge his bets and for the first time to recognise that he had two sons. He would have a grandchild in Kavanaugh House before he died, even if it meant that he had to acknowledge the bastard son he had denied until now.

Looking into Alyse's shocked green eyes across the table, Dario almost smiled, then clamped his mouth tight on the revealing expression. He had never anticipated getting married either. Had always vowed that it was not for him. When he'd come back to England this time, it had just been with the determination to thwart Marcus's plan. Then he would turn and walk away, for good this time. But then that letter had arrived and he had been offered the opportunity to take this one stage further than he had ever dreamed.

If he had known about that will sooner, then he might have had time to plan another approach to this, another way round it. But Marcus, damn his black soul, had made sure that he hadn't found out a thing until the very last minute, by which time his half-brother had already made his play for Alyse. He wasn't going to be wrong-footed again.

'Why won't it do?'

'Because Marcus doesn't want to put your father in jail—though he'll go that route if he has to. What he wants is you.'

'Oh, now you're...'

She was shaking her head violently so that the sleek blonde ponytail swung round, coming dangerously close to the candle flame. Dario leaned forward and moved it out of reach but then he stayed where he was, leaning halfway across the table, his face so much closer to hers.

'If you're going to tell me that I'm joking then I suggest you think again. Do you think that I would even be discussing this here tonight if there was any other alternative?'

Was it just the new shadows on her side of the room

or had she lost all colour completely, her eyes suddenly shockingly dark in contrast to the pale green of her dress?

'I—but—oh...'

One hand came up to her mouth, her fingers pressing against her lips to stop the awkward, uncertain flow of syllables. She still wore the pearly pink varnish on her nails and just the memory of those oval nails scraping over the skin of his palm, the longing to know that gentle rasp on other more intimate parts, had him hardening, fast and painful, so that he was grateful for the fact that his lower body was hidden under the protection of the table. Time enough for that later, when everything was settled. He couldn't afford to be distracted, to risk moving too fast and having her turn and run before everything was decided.

He saw the moment that she rallied and welcomed it. He wanted the proud, defiant Alyse he had seen on the night of the ball, when Marcus had thought he could call her to heel and had failed miserably. Trampling fragile, weak women underfoot did nothing for him. He left that sort of thing to Marcus. He might have the upper hand here and now—and he would use it to get what he wanted—but only because it was what Alyse wanted too. She just wasn't quite ready to admit it yet.

'I'm not stupid,' Alyse told him, a new flash of defiance in her eyes as they reflected the flicker of the candle flame. 'I know he fancies me—in fact, I'd go so far as to say he's been obsessed with me for some time. But I've given him no encouragement. Even though my father made it clear—for reasons I understand now—that he would welcome Marcus as a son-in-law. But I made it plain I wasn't interested.'

'Which, knowing Marcus, would only have made him more enthusiastic.'

Dario's mouth twisted cynically at the thought.

'He always wanted what he couldn't have—to deny him was the way to pique his interest.'

'That wasn't why I was doing it!'

'Do you think I don't know that? You were prepared to go to ridiculous extremes to get rid of his unwanted attention.'

Though she'd been quick enough to drop the whole idea once Marcus had interrupted things. He'd let her go that time. He'd never forced an unwilling woman and he didn't intend to start with Alyse Gregory. When she came to him—and she would come to him; there was no room at all for doubt about that—she would be as warm and willing as she had been in the heated, primitive dreams that had plagued his nights since that first meeting, heating his blood so much that he woke, damp with sweat, his heart pounding in arousal and it had taken a long cold shower to restore any sort of balance to his mind and body.

There were better ways of dealing with that burn of carnal arousal—and he reckoned that waiting would mean a more potent satisfaction in the end.

'You really don't know, do you?' he added when he saw the faint frown that drew her golden brows together, creasing the smooth skin of her forehead. 'You come with a perfect pedigree as far as Marcus—the whole Kavanaugh family—is concerned.'

'Pedigree? You make me sound like some sort of cat.'

'But only of the thoroughbred type.'

The deepening of her frown made Dario smile in response. Did she really still not get it? He liked that in her—that she didn't think of her title as something that anyone might find valuable.

'*Lady* Alyse...'

Understanding flashed over her face but she blinked hard, obviously not quite believing it.

'He thinks that matters?'

'His father does—enough to feel that a marriage to Your Ladyship would enhance the reputation of the family.'

It all made a sort of sense, Alyse supposed. If things like titles mattered so much—which it seemed they did for Marcus. It would explain why he had hounded her for so long. Before, he had just been an irritant, but now that he had this hold over her family...

But Marcus's father and Dario's father were one and the same man.

'Does that do it for you? The whole title thing?'

She saw the way his eyes narrowed sharply and wondered if she'd blundered in where she should have feared to tread. But then he laughed and leaned back in his seat again, reaching for his wineglass.

'Oh, *certamente*...' he drawled, something like real amusement warming his voice. 'Where I was dragged up, in the back streets of Casentino, we were obsessed with becoming lords and ladies—it was all we ever talked about.'

Alyse managed a smile because his comment was clearly meant to be humorous but she couldn't ignore the way it stung to think of him growing up as he had said.

'Your— Marcus's father didn't do anything to help you?'

It was like seeing his face turn to stone as she watched.

'Kavanaugh didn't acknowledge me—or my mother— for years. She was only some Italian peasant he had spent a drunken night with when he was staying with his wine supplier and she was working in the man's house. She tried to tell him she was pregnant but he refused to even see her.'

'What happened to your mother?'

'She died when I was fifteen.' The storm cloud that had

settled over his face grew darker with every word. 'I tried to get help from him when she became ill but...'

He flung up his hands in a gesture of dismissal, mouth clamped tight shut over whatever else he might have wanted to say.

'I'm sorry...'

She wanted to know how things had changed after that. Because they had changed somewhere in the past years. Dario was here now, obviously with some connection with his family, even if it wasn't on friendly terms. As she watched, Dario stood up and prowled across the room to the window and then back without looking out.

When he was this close he was so tall and imposing that she had a crick in her neck just looking up at him and the width of his shoulders blocked out the fading light from the window. Although he had said that he would help her, she didn't feel *safe* with him. Only in less danger than she had felt once she had known the truth about Marcus's scheming. The terrible fear that had crept over her when she had heard the full story from her father's lips, seen the pallor of his face, the shadows under his eyes had been almost more than she could bear, and if Dario would help her lift that then she would go with Dario—whatever the risks.

'If you marry me, then, as your husband, it will be my duty to help you and your family. And when your family's debts are paid then Marcus will have to leave you alone...'

'It's not that—' Put like that, it brought home to her all the more reason why she should feel this whole deal was just too good to be true. 'It's— What will you get out of this?'

Something changed in his blue eyes, like a wash of dark water flooding over them, but then, to her astonishment, they cleared again. Dario smiled down into her concerned face and, as he did so, he held out his hand to her, palm

upwards, as he had done when he had brought back the
pearl earring to her the day before. Dazedly, she put her
own hand into his and felt herself being drawn up to her
feet to stand close to him.

'Do you really have to ask?' he said, long fingers coming under her jaw, lifting her chin towards him, expos-
ing her mouth to his dark-eyed stare. That stare told her
what was coming and she wanted it; she welcomed it so
that she didn't know if she was the one who lifted her
face even closer or he bent his head to do the same. She
only knew that their mouths met perfectly, no hesitation,
no awkwardness.

After the heated passion of their first encounter she
was unprepared for the gentleness, the way that this kiss
seemed to draw out her soul and place it firmly in his
hands. Where that had been heat and fire, this was like
melting into the sun. She was adrift on a sensual sea, swaying on weakened legs, leaning into him, needing to be
closer...closer...pressed up tight against the hard muscled
lines of his body. His arms came round her, gathering her
even closer, hot, hard palms stroking down her back, burning through the pale linen of her dress. He cupped and held
the swell of her buttocks, lifting her so that she came into
even closer contact with the heated hardness between his
legs. The burn and pressure of it against her pelvis made
her pulse throb deep inside, the sting of arousal like an
electrical burn at her most feminine core.

'Dario...'

Unable to stop herself, she slithered closer, writhing
softly over the point of their intimate contact until she
heard him groan aloud in response and their mouths parted
enough to let him snatch in a hasty breath.

'*Strega...*' he muttered, stroking his right hand upwards
to where her breasts ached against him, the other broad

palm flattening across her bottom to hold her where he wanted her, where that intimate contact was inescapable. 'Witch!'

Well, if she was a witch then he was a sensual enchanter. He had barely kissed her half a dozen times and yet she was already desperate for his touch—for more. Knowing she would die if he didn't...

Her thoughts splintered into incoherence as that wandering hand closed, warm and strong, over the curve of her breast, cupping it through the fine fabric, setting her on fire all over again. She needed this.

'Bella strega,' Dario muttered against her lips once again, his tongue slipping along the seam of her mouth, teasing it open, tasting her. *'La mia bella strega.'*

It was so darkly sensual, so possessive that just for a second it was like a splash of cold water in her face, making her pull back an inch or two until she could meet the darkness of his eyes, seeing them hazed with the same passion that had put a flare of colour along those high, carved cheekbones.

'*Your* beautiful witch!' she managed in a voice that sparked with emotion—but whether with delight or indignation even she couldn't begin to tell.

She only knew that that possessive mutter had sliced into the heat haze that blurred her mind, bringing home to her just what this meant. That it wasn't the start of something wonderful, or just a one-night stand. It was the opening into the marriage that Dario had proposed—for purely business reasons.

'What is it?' Dario lifted his dark head, blue eyes searching into hers as if he wanted to read her mind. 'No second thoughts—no pretence.'

'I'm not...'

'And don't even try to claim this is not what you want

because I know when a woman is responding and any fool can see that you want me as much as I want you.'

Lifting the hand that had been tormenting her breast, he trailed the back of it softly down the side of her face, still watching intently, and smiled as he saw her shiver in uncontrollable response.

'My damn brother might have told you that he thought you were beautiful—that he wanted you until you were sick of it. But if I say it, then it will be true. I do think you are beautiful—I do *want* you, Alyse.'

Her name was a groan that pulled on something deep and primitive inside her soul.

'I want you so much that it's eating me up alive not to have you in my bed, not to possess you...'

There was no room for doubt on that point at least. The conviction in his voice, in his eyes, told its own story. He wanted her in a way that no one had ever wanted her in her life before. Being the child of an all-encompassing love like that between her parents meant that she had often felt as if she was on the outside, looking in, as now it seemed she had been, except for what they could get from her. She had never moved out of the house, into her own flat, because her mother needed her help and support. She was her mother's carer, her father's help. He had even tried to persuade her to accept Marcus's proposal because of the way it would rescue the family. But *this* was all for her.

I want you so much that it's eating me up alive...

She felt she could listen to him say that all night. No one had ever said anything like that to her before. Never made her feel so wanted before. The trouble was that she wished she could hear it for the rest of her life and she knew that was not what Dario had in mind. But she could have it for now. She could have that wild excitement, that feeling of being wanted more than any other woman alive that she had tasted so briefly on the night of the ball. She could have that and at the same time she would set her parents free from the fear and the impossible burden of debt that now hung round their necks.

'I want you too,' she acknowledged, too far gone to be able to lie even if she'd thought of it. She knew she was getting close to saying what he wanted to hear from her, teetering on the edge of giving in to him. But she still didn't know if it was safe.

And yet what other possible option did she have? The alternative was too terrible to consider.

'So you see why I'm doing this. You don't need to ask what I get from this bargain—the answer's obvious. I get you, in my bed, where I've wanted you from the first moment I saw you.'

And between them they rescued her father, saved her mother—and defeated Marcus. It was the only option she had so why not go with it?

What was so very different from the plan she had originally thought of—the path she had originally decided to take? That plan had been to win her freedom. A freedom she now needed more than ever.

Then she had been hunting for a way to win her freedom from Marcus's unwanted attentions. Now she wanted a far more basic liberty—the right to be her own person. She could never truly be that in her family home. She saw now that the near obsessive love her parents had left her no room to really be herself.

She'd planned that she would make it seem that she was attracted to someone else—that there was another man who could take Marcus's place and give her everything that she might have been forced to beg for from Dario's half-brother. Everything and more because she had never wanted Marcus as she hungered for Dario. He had never excited her, never aroused her just by a touch, a look. He had never promised her the open door into a world of wild passion, of sensual hunger and equally powerful sexual satisfaction.

And if her father went to prison, leaving her mother alone, then that was the end of her own dreams of freedom. She could never leave her mother to cope with the dangerous highs, the dreadful depressions that assailed her.

OK, so this wasn't the sort of marriage she had once dreamed of. But hadn't life shown her that that was just a fantasy anyway? Dario had made it plain that he wanted her, and he excited her, opened up new worlds to her. Wasn't that what she wanted for herself? Hadn't she come back to his apartment of her own volition on the night of the ball? Wouldn't she have been prepared to sleep with him—give herself to him without a single qualm? With the only thought in her head being the pleasure that she knew she would get from the encounter—the pleasure they would both give each other?

And if after that one night Dario had said that he wanted to see her again, that he wanted more, wanted the relationship to go on, she would have been up for it—wouldn't she? More than up for it—it would have been what she'd most wanted to hear. And she would have gone along with that happily.

So why was she balking at the word *marriage*? Because of her childhood dreams, the way that she had believed that her parents had the perfect relationship?

Her body knew what it wanted but if she fell into his arms now—into his bed—as she wanted to, what would happen then? When he'd had what he wanted why would he hang around, let alone do anything else to help her? Dario was offering her a way out. Everyone else had lied but he seemed to be totally straight with her.

'How do I know I can trust you? How do I know you'll keep your word? What is there to ensure that I get anything out of this and not just that you get all you want...?'

'And you don't want me?'

Soft and wicked as a snake's hiss, it left her floundering. But Dario didn't seem to need any answer as he smiled slow and wide.

'Will a contract suit you? A fully legal document—drawn up and signed by both of us? Our own private prenup—with the conditions and benefits spelled out clear and precise. What we each get out of this and what we'll have when it's over and done with. When the marriage breaks up and we each go our separate ways.'

But what would he get out of it? Apart from the satisfaction of thwarting his half-brother. Would that be enough? Certainly, it seemed that Dario loathed Marcus enough to make it worth his while to go through this pretence of a marriage.

That and the fact that he would get the other thing he desired—her in his bed, where he had wanted her, he said, from the moment he had first seen her. It made her mouth dry, set her head into a spin. She didn't know whether the wildness inside was the result of fear or the delirium of sexual hunger that Dario somehow seemed to be able to spark off in her just by existing.

Was that enough to satisfy a man like Dario? Was she enough to satisfy him?

'It'll have to be signed, sealed, completely watertight—everything spelled out, every last detail. No loopholes...'

'You can instruct my lawyer yourself,' Dario replied, totally unfazed by her demand. 'And of course you don't have to sign anything until you're completely satisfied.'

He made it sound so fair, so completely reasonable—as if she could have any and everything she wanted. As if this truly was a contract between equals, giving and receiving on both sides. And yet she knew that that was just not the case.

Dario was the one who got what he wanted. She was the one with so much to lose. If she didn't sign then Dario could just walk away, sexually frustrated perhaps, but not truly damaged. She would be left in the nightmare her life had just turned into—with her mother desperately ill— because surely this would plunge her into deeper, darker depths than she had ever sunk to before. And her father would be in prison for crimes he had only committed to protect the woman he loved.

It was just too horrific. It would destroy them both.

She had the opportunity to help them as she had the courage to take it. And at the end of it—whenever that end came—she would have the freedom she most longed for.

She sucked in a deep, strengthening breath, swallowed hard.

'See your lawyer then,' she said and was relieved to hear that her voice sounded strong enough to convince anyone that she was perfectly at ease with her decision. 'Get this contract drawn up, then bring it to me and I'll sign it. And let's get this show on the road.'

Dark triumph flared in Dario's eyes, in his smile.

'Then come here—'

He reached for her again, and just the feel of his hand closing around the bare skin of her arm set all those wild, yearning sensations spiralling in the pit of her stomach.

It was too much like the way it had been on the night of the ball. Too close to that moment when he had crowed over Marcus, telling his half-brother that he had lost while Dario had won. She didn't want it to be like that; didn't want to go back to being the bone tugged between the two snarling, angry dogs. This was something different—

something new—and she wanted it to stay that way. She wanted to be more in control than before.

'No...' She managed to put a teasing note into it, even added a smile and a brief, light kiss to the tip of his nose. 'Not until our wedding night.'

'How very old-fashioned of you.' She didn't know how to interpret the intonation he put on that.

'Well, that's me—an old-fashioned kind of girl.'

She turned a slanting, coquettish glance on him in an attempt to dissipate the storm clouds she could see gathering in those sapphire eyes. 'Oh, don't worry—you'll get what you've paid for—but not until the ring is on my finger.'

She'd gone a step—several steps—too far there. Those clouds hadn't evaporated. If anything, they'd grown darker, deeper. Now she waited, breath catching in her throat as he studied her face, considering his answer. Inwardly she tensed, expecting a nuclear explosion. To her relief, it didn't come.

'All right then, *mia strega*—we'll do this the traditional way. Not until our wedding night—*but then...*'

He let the sentence trail off but he didn't need to say it. She could fill in the spaces herself and her mind threatened to blow a fuse under the impact of the wild, sensual images of the night ahead of her.

'I'll see my lawyer tomorrow—get that pre-nup drawn up as soon as possible. Because I don't intend to wait for you, *bellissima.*'

It was only what she'd expected. Alyse felt a blend of excitement and apprehension bubbling up inside her. She couldn't believe that this stunning, devastating man could want her so much that he would go to these lengths to get her. Even to tying himself into a marriage of convenience that was going to cost him a small fortune as a bride price.

Deep inside she felt a new kind of thrill, a quiver of rare, stinging excitement at the thought.

But then he dropped her right back down to earth by adding bluntly, 'I want you in my bed before the month is out—or sooner. Marcus won't wait for what he's owed—and neither will I.'

CHAPTER SIX

'You look lovely!'

'Thank you, Dad.'

Alyse managed to respond to her father's comment with a smile that frayed slightly at the edges. She had to be thankful that her father was smiling too, and he seemed almost ten years younger than he had done two weeks ago. With the huge debt he'd owed completely paid, and the threat of imprisonment now only a bad memory, he looked as if a huge weight had been lifted from his shoulders. No tears now, but Ellen had already been sniffing sentimentally into a handkerchief before she had left for the church. But at least they had been happy tears and there had been a new lightness in her step as she'd headed for the car.

'You are sure—you're happy?' he asked now, his expression grave as he searched her face for the truth. 'It is all very sudden.'

Now he asked! Now he was concerned! The words stung at Alyse's brain and she had to bite down hard on her lower lip to stop herself from letting them escape.

'Sudden but right!' she said as warmly as she could.

She hoped she hid it well, and that her smile was convincing. She had made Dario agree that they would let her parents think that this love affair was real, if sudden and overwhelming. The rush to get married was because of

the passionate way they felt about each other—and Dario
had determined to show his love for his prospective bride
by paying off her family's debts.

But the truth was that none of this felt real to Alyse. It
was as if she was functioning on the other side of a huge
sheet of plate glass so that she could see her parents, talk
to them, hear their responses, but she wasn't really *with*
them. She could no longer see them as she had done before.
Once she'd realised the truth about the way that they had
both been involved in almost forcing her into a marriage
to Marcus she didn't want, she had seemed to step back
from them, putting a distance between them that right now
she couldn't bridge. At the same time, Dario was the one
person who felt fully real to her. He was the person she
had chosen, the one with whom she had thrown in her lot.
Her future lay with him for as long as it lasted.

Already she was moving away from her parents towards
a life that was at last her own. Or at least the one she had
chosen for now. It might be just a business arrangement,
but Dario hadn't realised how important a gift he was giving her in her freedom.

'Yes, it's a lightning romance, Dad, but sometimes that
happens. You'd only known Mum for a month but you always told me that...'

'I knew she was the one for me.' Her father nodded his
agreement.

'So there you are—lightning strikes and you are left
with no choice.' Alyse slid her arm through his, grateful
for the strength and support. She had only to get through
today and...

The thought of what lay ahead at the end of the day almost ruined her determined attempt to look confident and
happy. It was one thing to play the happy fiancée for the
past couple of weeks, quite another to know that she and

Dario would be alone tonight and for many more nights to come.

Just the thought made her mouth dry painfully.

It was crazy but the closer today had come, the more she had felt her nerves tighten into painful knots of apprehension. At the start of the fourteen days before their wedding was to take place, she'd thought it would be so hard to play the devoted fiancée but in the end it had been ridiculously easy. Dario strolled through the performance with a quick, easy smile here, a lingering touch there. If they stood close together he hooked his arm around her waist, drawing her closer. His fingers often tangled in the fall of her hair and, if her parents were near, he stole sneaky kisses, pretending to be shy or diffident about showing the way he felt in front of her mother and father.

Which was ridiculous. She doubted that Dario Olivero had ever had a diffident day in his whole life. And she had the evidence of his blazing kisses, the sensual touch that seared a protective layer of skin from her body every time it touched her, the heated caresses that aroused her in a heartbeat.

But, strangely, it was those less forceful touches that scorched right through to her soul and made her want him, need him more than ever before. If she could have done so without backing down from her insistence that they wait until their wedding night, she would have grabbed him by both of those tantalising hands and dragged him off upstairs to her bedroom, never caring who was watching. But the one time she had tried it, it had been Dario who had held back. Dario who had eased himself away from her clinging grip, who had shaken his head slowly, almost regretfully, and leaned forward to press a lingering, enticing kiss just beside her right ear.

'Not until our wedding night,' he had whispered softly,

the smile on his lips communicating itself to her through the warmth of his breath against her sensitive skin. 'I promised.'

He had enjoyed himself by keeping that promise whilst driving her to distraction as a result. She had almost been driven to beg, but the knowledge that he would enjoy refusing her had kept the words from her tongue when they had almost escaped.

But *tonight*... Tonight he would have the right to possess her body as fully and as often as he wanted. And it was that 'right' that weakened her blood, made her legs feel like cotton wool beneath her.

'Ready?' her father whispered, pausing at the door into the church to squeeze her hand.

'Ready.' Alyse nodded, though she doubted if that was quite the right word. If someone could be ready and yet totally unready at the same time, then that was how she felt at this moment.

Looking down at her hand where it rested on her father's arm, she couldn't miss the gleam of the brilliant diamond ring Dario had given her.

'I don't need it!' she'd protested when he'd slid it onto her finger just before they had gone together to tell her parents about their marriage. 'It's only for show.'

That had earned her a dark frown and a reproving glare.

'None of this is for show,' he'd growled. 'At least not where Marcus and Henry Kavanaugh are concerned. We might know about the agreement we have, but no one else ever will. Everyone must think that this is for real. And, to ensure that, we have to do things properly.'

There was 'proper' and then there was this stonking great gem that flashed and sparkled, emblazoning their association in the most blatant way. And it was made all the worse by the fact that somehow he had found out about her love for vintage jewellery and the brilliant diamond could never have been matched in any modern design. This was so much the sort of glorious jewellery she might have chosen for herself—if she could possibly ever have afforded it—that it took her breath away.

'Come on, love,' her father urged, bringing home to her the fact that she had been hesitating too long, not taking a single step forward towards the altar. If she wasn't careful she was going to give away the fact that this was not at all the real love match it was meant to be.

'Let's go.'

Her feet felt unsteady as she walked, the floor seeming to rock beneath her so that she felt disturbingly seasick. She clutched at her father's arm, put all her weight on him as she gathered her breath, trying to force her eyes to focus so that she could see straight.

But seeing straight meant that she could see where Dario stood, tall and proud, shoulders squared, long back perfectly straight, at the end of the aisle. She couldn't see his face, of course, so there was no way to read what he was feeling. Nothing like as nervous as she was, that much was obvious. But did he think that this was worth it—that marrying her was worth all he had paid for her?

Alyse wished that he would turn round. That she could see his stunning face and remind herself...

The thought evaporated in a second as Dario did exactly as she had wished, turning his dark head to glance back over his shoulder. That one second where their gazes met, clashed, shook her world from top to bottom. Of course he was here. He was a businessman and he had organised this business deal so obviously he was going to see it through to the end. He was known for being ruthless, unyielding, never wavering until he had what he wanted. So why that quick, unsmiling, dark-eyed check over his shoulder to watch her approach?

Had he doubted that she would come here today? Not Dario—how could he ever doubt that? She was his investment. His stake in the deal. He would know that she had no alternative but to come here today or see her parents destroyed.

They had reached Dario's side now. Was it her imagination or did he seem taller, bigger, more powerful as he took a step closer? The formal morning coat fitted him to perfection, but with the restraint of it, the elegant crisp white shirt and silvery-grey cravat, he seemed so much more distant, alien to her. She didn't know this man and yet she was signing away her life into marriage with him. Panic fluttered like a trapped butterfly halfway up her throat, so that she needed to gasp in air to relieve the sensation.

She felt her father ease her hand from his arm, pass it into Dario's keeping, but she couldn't look at him, couldn't look anywhere but into those probing blue eyes. His hand closed around hers, warm and strong, but, frighteningly, it felt like imprisonment rather than support.

'Thank you...'

She heard her father's heartfelt words to the man who would soon become his son-in-law. In spite of herself, she couldn't help wondering whether he would have said the same to her at just this moment if she had agreed to marry Marcus. Or was it just Dario who he saw as his rescuer?

Rose, acting as her senior bridesmaid, eased the bouquet of lilies from her nerveless spare hand but Alyse barely noticed them go. She couldn't look anywhere but at Dario, couldn't register anything but the warmth and strength of his body beside her. The scent of his skin and some cool, crisp cologne reached out to enclose her but she couldn't register any of the sensuality that had been her response on so many other occasions. This felt all wrong—so cold, so calculated. So dangerous. And Dario himself stood taut and inflexible, as if he was armouring himself against any feelings the place and the event might create. He was not going to ease up, not going to *give*. He was here to receive his due—the conqueror who was entitled to his prize and he was going to take it.

'You look beautiful.'

The intonation on the last word was so unexpected that she jumped in reaction and felt his hand tighten around hers just for a moment. She couldn't miss the way that his assessing gaze slid over her hair, left loose under the delicate coronet of flowers in white and gold, took in her face and moved on down to the simple white dress. He almost controlled his reaction but she saw the way his mouth tightened and his eyes narrowed.

'Th-thank you. I—'

She wanted to explain about the dress. She guessed that she knew what he was thinking under that unmoving expression. He was wondering what had happened to the couture gown he had expected her to wear, created by the designer he'd sent to her. It must be obvious, even to a man, that the simple sleeveless sheath that clung to every slender curve was not the creation of the French designer he had chosen.

'I...'

She opened her mouth to speak. But the celebrant had stepped forward and begun to speak and the moment was lost.

She did look beautiful. Dario tried to focus on what the priest was saying but it was impossible to clear his head from the first impressions he had of Alyse as she'd walked down the aisle towards him, taken her place at his side.

He didn't know what he'd been expecting, but it was not this. Oh, he'd known she would be beautiful; she could never be anything but. From the first moment he'd seen her from across the room at the ball, she had knocked him off balance and he'd never been able to think straight since. At least not where she was concerned.

'If any person present knows of any lawful impediment...'

The celebrant's voice tuned in and then out of his hearing like a faulty radio receiver. If anyone did decide to say there was a reason why they should not marry, then he wouldn't hear it. But, all the same, the words were echoing over and over inside his head.

Damn it to hell, didn't he, of all people, know why they shouldn't marry?

Why they shouldn't go through with this travesty of a wedding—this making of vows in a church, before a priest—it went against all he believed a marriage should be.

Oh, not for him. He'd never considered marriage for himself; he just wasn't made for it. But as an institution... as the dream that his mother had longed for all her life and never even come close to, it could mean—should mean— a great deal.

Just for a moment he let it drift through his head to question what might happen if he said that, yes, he knew of a reason why they should not be joined together. Would his mother's ghost rest any happier then?

Because his mother was part of why he was doing this. It might be too late, but perhaps, even now, he could give her her greatest wish, if only posthumously. She had always dreamed of seeing her son in Kavanaugh House, where she'd believed he belonged, inheriting his father's name in that way at least. But he also knew that she had always wanted him to marry for love.

Alyse hadn't asked for love. It had all been about the money and getting bloody Marcus off her back, once and for all. That hadn't been any sort of a lie. Marcus would not have been deterred by anything except a formal marriage contract, signed and sealed and legally unbreakable. As to the other results that this marriage could bring, that was between him and his father.

In that moment as silence descended as the celebrant finished '...or for ever hold your peace...' Alyse shifted slightly beside him, her hand trembling in his.

Immediately he looked down at her, just in the same moment that she lifted her face to look up at him and he saw the faint quiver of her mouth, the huge darkness of her green eyes. Hell, but she was beautiful...

But this whole event was not at all what he'd been expecting. No matter who she was marrying, and even if the ceremony had been arranged in what many might think was indecent haste, the wedding of Lady Alyse Gregory was a society event. One that might have been expected to be celebrated with show and formality. He'd been prepared to pay for that. Instead, it had turned out to be this pared-down, simple event in the village church near where Alyse had grown up.

She had even turned down the offer of a designer to create her dress. And when he had expected no-expense-spared, glamorous style, the simple silk sheath she wore was a major shock and not one he was comfortable with. He didn't like the way it made him feel.

His fingers tightened around the hand in his. It felt ridiculously small, delicate in his hold. The simplicity of her dress, the understated make-up and hair, brought words he'd never wanted into his head. Words like *vulnerable* and *gentle*. Words he'd never connected with any woman before—and wasn't at all sure how he felt about connecting them with this one, here and now, in these circumstances.

'Dario?' The priest was smiling, looking into his face, and it startled him back to the present.

He'd missed his cue. Missed the moment where he'd been asked, 'Do you take this woman…?' and now everyone was watching, waiting for him to give his answer.

Alyse's hand twitched nervously as if she was about to pull away and in hasty response he clamped his fingers tight around hers again, holding her still. He wasn't going to let this fail, not this close to the finishing line.

'I do,' he said, firm and strong, and could almost feel the visible relaxation of the congregation in the church behind him. A quick glance down to the woman beside him saw the way her eyes had widened in shock and concern. Had she really believed that he wouldn't go through with this? But then she only knew the half of it. The half that affected her directly.

'Alyse…'

It was her turn to be asked that question. Her response came quicker, sharper as if she wanted it said; needed it done.

He'd treat her right, he promised the spectre of his mother, who haunted his thoughts. She'd get everything she wanted out of this. After all, what she wanted was easy to provide. Money, first and foremost, and freedom for her parents. Freedom for her from Marcus's damned pursuit of her. And the sexual fulfilment that would come from them being in bed together. The consummation of desire that he'd been hungry for from the first moment he'd seen her.

Just the thought of it made his grip on her hand tighten, the pressure of skin on skin a silent promise to her—and to himself—of what was to come.

'I do...'

They were the words Alyse had been worrying about ever since she'd woken this morning. Just two simple words but they'd spun round and round in her thoughts, threatening to drive her crazy. Two words to change her life. Once she'd said those two words, there was no going back. She would be married to Dario and their pre-nuptial contract would become legal and binding.

That was what she wanted, wasn't it? If she didn't go through with this then her parents would suffer and she would never know the truth of Dario's lovemaking. The dreams that she had of him during the night, erotic dreams that still clung to her mind like thick, sticky cobwebs, and left her damp with sweat, her bed a mess of tangled sheets, told her how much her body hungered for his. And tonight...

Her mind hazed at the realisation that she was thinking of hot, passionate sex right here, before the altar, with her hand tight in Dario's.

He hadn't let go of her hand. If anything, he held it tighter, and didn't let go all through the vital questions. Did he think that she might run away? That she might escape him and leave him with her part of the bargain unpaid? He'd already made good on his promises. She knew, because her father had been bubbling over with the news that all those terrible debts had been paid.

So was she the only possible loose end he felt might escape him? Did he think that perhaps she would dodge out of what she owed him and run for her life?

Something disturbingly close to her heart ached at the thought. She couldn't...she wouldn't.

'I do...' she said again, unthinkingly, and heard the ripple of amusement from the pews behind her at her apparent need to emphasise the point.

There was no echoing smile in Dario's dark face, though. His expression was sombre, unrevealing, and his eyes like bottomless dark pools, threatening to drown her in their depths.

Somehow she made it through the rest of the service. The vows were made, the ring was on her finger—another bigger, broader one on his, and they were now pronounced to be man and wife.

'You may kiss the bride...' just about registered in her numbed brain as Dario swept her off her feet in a huge enveloping hug, lifting her to meet his mouth as he crushed his hard lips against hers in a fiercely overwhelming kiss.

The unexpected display of passion knocked all the breath out of her body and had her clinging to him for support, glorying in the feel of his strength surrounding her, the play of powerful muscles under the expensive material of his morning coat, the scent of his skin blending with the tang of some citrus and bergamot cologne. She could do this! Oh, dear heaven, she *wanted* to do this!

The moment seemed to go on for ever but, at long last, Dario released her, taking his mouth from hers and letting her slide slowly back down until her toes were on the floor. Which meant that her ear was just level with his mouth.

'Now let anyone claim that this isn't for real,' he muttered, clearly taking a dark satisfaction in the way that a ripple of applause spread through the church. 'Welcome to my life, Signora Olivero.'

Why didn't he just say 'Welcome to my bed'? Alyse wondered. Because that had been all there was in that kiss. Passion, primal, sexual need—but nothing else. If he had taken her out and branded her as his, he couldn't have made a more blatant statement of possession. He had got what he wanted—and she would be all kinds of a fool if she tried to read anything more into it.

Somehow she managed to make her way back down the aisle, her hand tucked into Dario's arm to support her. She exchanged smiles with her family, her friends, and it was only then that it was brought home to her just how much the congregation was weighted in her favour, with just a few friends who had come from Italy to be with Dario today.

As he walked at her side Dario stood tall and proud and, although he turned his head, nodded to acknowledge the congratulations of everyone, there was a distinct tension about him, one that only she was aware of. If she glanced up at his face, she saw that the smiles that came and went like a flashing neon sign did nothing to reach his eyes while that narrowed blue gaze was flicking around the church, looking left and right as if he was searching for someone.

Whoever it was, he didn't find them. They got to the end of the aisles and then out into the sunshine without there being any moment when he registered anyone special. It was shocking how lonely that made her feel for him. His mother had died, he'd said, and of course the one member of his family that she really knew about—Marcus—was hardly likely to be at the celebration of this particular wedding.

'I'm sorry—' she said, unable to hold back as they snatched a moment alone, waiting for everyone else to come out of the church behind them.

'Sorry?'

The look he turned on her was unfocused and opaque, totally without any emotion.

'My family—they did rather monopolise the church—and you—'

'Why should that matter?' He frowned. 'It is how it is.'

'But you...' she tried again, stumbling to a halt as he

shook his head in rejection of her attempt to reach out to him.

'It's nothing, Alyse. Nothing matters but us. I don't do family.'

At that moment the light wind blew a large white cloud in front of the sun, blocking out its warmth and making Alyse shiver in sudden response. But it was more the effect of Dario's words that had struck home to her rather than the sudden chill. They sounded not just as some explanation for the effect the past had on the present—but also as a cold-blooded decree for the prospect of the future.

CHAPTER SEVEN

'I CAN'T REALLY believe I'm here...'

Alyse shaded her eyes against the burn of the setting sun as she stared out at the beauty of the countryside that surrounded them. The view from the stone terrace of the huge villa was spectacular. Away towards the horizon were some of the vineyards Dario owned.

'Why not?' Dario's tone was sharp.

The truth was that she'd never thought he'd take her to his home. Dario was a man who valued his privacy—the limited amount he'd told her about his life, his past, made that plain. So she had never expected to be whisked away from the reception and hurried onto a private jet for the flight to Tuscany. Now this unexpected insight into the private and personal life of the man she had married left her feeling as if her feet weren't quite on solid ground.

'I never thought we'd have a honeymoon,' she said hastily, not wanting him to see the truth in her face.

Things were inside out. They should have been doing this—learning about each other—*before* the wedding ceremony. Now here she was realising just how little she knew about the man the world would call her husband. The man whose bed she would share tonight and every night for however long this marriage of convenience would last.

'I said we'd do things properly.'

'So you did.' She hoped that her smile didn't look as forced as it felt. How could he make a statement sound like a reproach? 'And everything was completely—proper.'

It was strange how different that word could sound, the subtle way its meaning varied. Everything about the day had been totally appropriate for a hasty, passionate, romantic wedding. But no one could ever have described the events that had led up to this marriage-business fusion as being 'proper' in the way that usually had the word 'prim' in front of it. How would everyone in the church—her family—have felt if they'd known that basically she had sold herself to Dario for an appalling amount of money? The reasons behind it didn't really change anything. There was an ugly word for what she'd done.

'It was wonderful, all of it.'

She didn't need to force any enthusiasm into her voice as she turned to face him. With the formal wear of the day discarded for something more suited to the warmer temperatures in Tuscany, he was now wearing a loose white shirt, sleeves rolled up to expose the length of his arms, and well-worn faded denim jeans. Once they'd reached the villa he'd even kicked off his shoes and now padded barefoot along the sun-warmed terrace. Against the rosy brickwork of the building behind him, its colour enhanced by the glow of the burning sunset, his monochrome form looked stark and dangerous. But he had been so generous, more than she had ever had the right to ask of him.

'A very special day.' A couple of hasty steps took her close enough to press a spontaneous kiss against his lean cheek, roughened by the long day's growth of dark stubble. 'I know everyone thought so too.'

'I can't say I give a damn about what everyone else thought,' Dario muttered roughly. 'So long as you enjoyed your day.'

'Oh, I did!'

Alyse didn't let herself consider his choice of words. *Your day,* not *our day*—or even just *the day*—as if he had no part in it, other than paying for every damn thing, of course.

'It was lovely—thank you.'

Her lips were still just inches away from his face; she could smell his skin, taste him on her mouth, and her eyes were locked with his sapphire ones that had now turned a deeper, darker blue, Her stomach flipped over, her pulse heating and setting her blood pounding.

'I'm sure I'll find it was worth it.'

It took a stunned second or two for the full meaning of his words to hit home and make her heart clench tight in apprehension but in the same moment she already knew that she didn't care. He might call this the recompense for all he had paid out, the return that he had paid for, but there was more to it than that for Alyse. This was pure sensuality, a deep and darkly primal need that flooded through her as she pressed her mouth to his cheek again, feeling the scrape of bristle, the heat of flesh, the tightness of a strong muscle that jerked underneath her kiss.

'That you're worth it.'

A sudden swift movement and it was not his cheek that she was kissing but the full burning pressure of his mouth on hers. His kiss had no give to it but took and demanded as clearly he believed he was entitled to do.

He *was* entitled. This was what she'd promised him. But from the moment that his mouth collided with hers she knew that she didn't give a damn. This wasn't just about what Dario had bought and paid for. It was what she wanted; what they both wanted and now was the time. The fire they had lit between them might have smouldered slowly for some time, pushed underneath by circumstances, by Alyse's decree that she wanted to wait until their wedding night, but right now it flared into wild flame in the space of a heartbeat, searing hot and hungry through both of them.

'I've waited long enough for this,' Dario muttered harshly against her mouth, tilting her head back with the force of his kiss so that the setting sun burned into her eyes. 'Too damn long.'

'Too damn long,' Alyse echoed on a sigh of acquiescence.

In this moment she had no idea why she had ever imposed that crazy sanction. Why she had ever thought it was important that he should wait—that they both should wait. This was what she'd wanted then; what she wanted now and the intervening two weeks had only made the hunger so much harder to bear.

Flinging her arms up around Dario's neck, she tangled her fingers in the jet-black silk of his hair, feeling the burn of need pulse deep inside her.

'Too damn long,' she repeated with even more emphasis.

She felt the sardonic laughter that shook his powerful frame like a new sensation against her skin, an unexpected caress that crushed the fine linen of her turquoise sundress against breasts that already felt tight and hot, hungry for his touch.

'So why the hell...?'

She pushed the rest of his question back down his throat with the force of her own kiss.

'Because I could,' she told him sassily. 'And because I was a fool.'

'Too damn right you were a fool—and I was a bigger one to agree. But not any more.'

His hands were busy at the back of her dress, tugging at the zip, dragging it down to expose the line of her spine, but at the same time he managed to swing her off her feet and up into his arms. The hand that supported her back slid in between her dress and her skin, smoothing over fine bones, adding heat where she was already burning, hunger where she was already so needy.

'Not any more,' she managed because all she could do was to echo his rough-voiced statement. It was exactly the way she felt.

She had only the most basic knowledge of the villa. They had arrived less than an hour earlier, their bags taken to their room by some unseen member of staff. Then Dario had suggested a glass of wine on the terrace so she had no idea where they were going, but it didn't matter. Dario was in charge and Dario knew exactly where he was going.

With each step they mounted on the way upstairs, he paused, dragging another kiss from her lips, crushing her against the wall to hold her exactly where he wanted her. The plaster of the wall was cool against her skin, a stunning contrast to the raging fire at the points where her body was crushed up against his, and the even fiercer one that burned deep inside, just inches away from the hot caress of his hand.

'This is what it's all been about.'

Dario's tone was thick and rough, each word punctuated by another greedy, snatching kiss, crushing her mouth, taking her soul. One of her sandals slipped from her feet and tumbled down the stairs, followed almost immediately by the other. Alyse heard the sound as a drum roll of inexorable passion. Inescapable and unstoppable. This had been inevitable from the moment they had met and she didn't want to delay another second. She had managed to get her hands between them, ripping open his shirt so wildly that buttons spun off and dropped to the floor. She thrilled by the feel of his hard, warm chest, lightly hazed with crisp, dark hair beneath her fingers. She scraped her nails over the beautiful olive skin, feeling his heart kick in response, his groan of need making her smile against his shoulder.

When Dario kicked open a door at the top of the stairs her heart jumped so wildly that she could hardly breathe. Her blood was pounding in her ears as he carried her across the room, dropped her with little ceremony onto a downy white duvet on top of the bed. Hating the feeling of separation, the breath of cold air that came between them, she moaned a complaint, reaching for him at once.

'*Momento...*'

He was throwing off his clothes, his shirt already half off after her urgent attentions. It was dropped to the floor, his trousers and black boxer shorts following swiftly. Then he bent over her, taking her mouth again, nipping, sucking, tracing his tongue along the join of her lips, enticing his way inside to taste her more intimately. Alyse was already trying to shrug herself out of her dress, the top half gaping wide to expose the peach silk and lace of her bra, the flushed curves of her breasts.

'Now—now...Dario...'

'No—wait...'

Wait! Her body screamed the hungry reproach but already Dario had turned his head, the heat and weight of his long body holding her imprisoned on the bed as he tugged open a drawer in a nearby bedside cabinet. After a moment's stunned confusion, Alyse realised what was going on.

'No need...'

She reared up to whisper the words in his ear.

'I'm safe...in all ways.'

'Safe?'

He spared her a glance, though it was obvious that he had to fight against his body's needs to do so. Already the heated thrust of his penis was hard against her thighs, but still he held away from her even though she opened her legs beneath him.

'Best to be sure.'

'I am...'

But already he was sheathing himself, his movements firm and competent, turning kisses on her pouting mouth as he set out to distract her, keep her hungry at the same time.

'So am I—now...'

It was rough and raw, deep in his throat as his teasing mouth moved lower, tongue trailing over her peaking breasts, his teeth closing over the edges of her bra, tugging it down so that his tongue could slide over the delicate skin he had exposed. Then he closed his lips over the pouting nipple, sucking on her through the silk and letting his teeth scrape across the distended flesh, tugging softly.

'Damn you...damn you...' Alyse muttered, cursing him for the delay and yet unable to resist the stinging pleasure of his mouth.

She writhed beneath him, open and hungry, and yearning for the fulfilment his passion promised.

'Come into me, Dario,' she whispered against his ear. 'Take me—make this real...'

She broke off on a high, sighing cry of completion as he moved his big body, slid inside her, pushing deeper and deeper until she felt totally filled, totally given up to him.

'So right...' she sighed. 'So—so right.'

'So right,' Dario agreed, his voice rough and uneven, as he started to move, to press in and out, taking, giving, putting himself totally into her arms as she closed them around him, held his strength tight against her.

Alyse was lost, adrift on the heated waves of passion that swept over her, taking her higher, higher, faster and faster. She felt her muscles bunching, contracting, gathering themselves towards the fulfilment she was reaching for. She was gripping Dario tight, abandoning herself to him, throwing her head back and letting his name escape on a moan of need as he quickened his pace, thrust into her again and again.

'Dario... Oh, Dario!'

She was totally focused, totally lost, abandoning herself to him as the convulsions of delight broke over her, driving her beyond reality into the force of the starburst of pleasure that exploded all around her, forcing the wild, high cry of his name from her lips as she gave herself up to it.

It was a long, heated, sensual night, one that left them sated with each other's bodies, abandoned to exhaustion in the end when they could physically take no more. It was early morning when Alyse finally stirred, stretching and staring around her sleepily, acknowledging the ache of muscles tired by the night's activities, the faint soreness where love bruises marked her skin.

As Dario stirred lazily beside her, rubbing his face into the pillow as he woke, she noticed the aftermath of their passion, the garments discarded here, there and everywhere on the floor where they had tossed them aside in their rush to fulfilment. Stretching out a lazy hand, she reached for her own clothing and surveyed it ruefully.

'You tore my dress.'

She held up the turquoise linen dress or, rather, the remains of it. It was ripped from top to bottom, coming apart at the seams.

The look Dario turned on it was careless, indifferent, but shaded with a rich seam of dark triumph.

'It was in the way.' He lifted those powerful shoulders—shoulders that were now marked with the attentions of her hands, her nails, even her teeth. 'I'll buy you another one.'

Lazy, hazy blue eyes, still filled with the after-effects of the mind-blowing passion that had taken them by storm, mocked her indignation, and his smile was even more slow and indulgent.

'And then I'll rip that one off you too. But I have to admit that I prefer you as you are now...'

His gaze slid over her naked body, caressing the flushed lines of her cheeks, the curve of her shoulders, her breasts above the fine cotton sheet she had pulled over her as she sat up. A moment later an equally caressing hand followed the same route. Smoothing her skin, curving over her breast, cupping its weight in his palm.

'Yes,' he drawled softly, 'this is how I'd like you to stay for the rest of your life.'

'A little impractical.' Alyse's voice was tight with the effort she was making not to respond to his touch.

'Who gives a damn about practical?' Dario's hands were now curved under her breasts, his thumbs toying with the nipples, still pink and tender from his earlier attentions. Alyse shivered as his slightly roughened pads rubbed across the swollen skin, sending burning arrows of need shooting down to pool with moist heat between her legs. 'This marriage is not about practical. It's about this...'

Another sweep of his thumbs, harder this time, had her throwing back her head and gasping in air.

'Isn't it...?'

This time he rolled her nipples between his fingers, blue eyes very dark as he watched intently, his mouth just curling at the corners as he saw her response.

'Isn't it, *bellissima*?'

Alyse threw caution to the winds. To hell with restraint—and with anything else! Who cared if he thought she was a total pushover where he was concerned? That was the exact truth, wasn't it? So why was she trying to hide it from him? It only delayed the pleasure and the satisfaction she was now longing for all over again. And she didn't want to delay for any reason.

'Yes,' she whispered, low and hungry.

'I can't hear you.'

Deliberately provoked and not giving a damn about it, she let her eyes fly open, stunned to find that he had moved closer and his mouth was almost touching hers. She had only to speak to taste his skin against hers but she wanted more than that.

'Yes, damn you—yes!'

This time she took the initiative, almost throwing herself at him, taking his mouth with hers as she pressed him down onto the bed, flat underneath her.

'Yes...'

She kissed him hard and long, her hands making slow sensual forays along the length of his body, her mouth smiling against his as she felt the way the powerful muscles bunched and jerked under her touch.

'Oh, yes...'

She let her fingers tiptoe over his burning skin, along the hair-roughened length of his thigh to where the neediest part of him strained against her, hard and hungry as before. When she drifted her touch over him she felt him jump beneath her teasing torment, a rush of Italian curses spilling from his lips.

'Now what was that you were saying about pleasure?' she teased, looking down into his face where deep dark eyes glazed with passion, high cheekbones were heavily marked with the burn of need.

Her hands moved again, stroking, tormenting, squeezing lightly till she felt him buck hard underneath her.

'Was this what you meant?'

'Almost!' His voice was rough and raw, cracking at the edges.

'Almost?'

She barely had the time to get the word out, no chance to wonder what he might mean, when he grabbed her hands in a bruising grip, yanked them away from their tormenting journey. Holding her arms wide, he used his greater strength to twist himself out from underneath her, turning her upside down as he did. When she landed on her back on the bed, he was there, on top of her, crushing her down into the soft mattress before she had time even to breathe, let alone speak.

'Almost,' he grated again. '*Quasi, la mia bella strega.* But this…'

He brought her hands up over her head, held them firmly on the pillow, one of his larger hands holding both her wrists imprisoned tight as he pushed his knee between her thighs, opening her up to him as his lips tormented her aching nipple, suckling and nibbling, drawing into the heat and moistness of his mouth.

'This,' he repeated, coming into her with one hard, forceful thrust, making her toss her head against the pillows in heated delight as she felt the power and strength of him stretching the muscles that were so ready, so hungry for him there.

'*This* is what I meant.'

CHAPTER EIGHT

'TALKING OF DRESSES...'

Some time early in the morning, when the faint rays of dawn were just beginning to creep over the horizon seen from the unshuttered windows, Dario stirred again sleepily, twisting on his side to reach down and snatch up the tangled remnants of the turquoise dress from where it lay on the bed. Flopping back onto the pillows, he held it up, threading it through his bronzed fingers.

'What was wrong with the wedding dress Lynette designed for you?'

He said it casually but, because she had known that this was coming, she felt her stomach muscles tighten, the lazy, satisfied warmth seeping away in an instant.

'The one you wanted me to wear.' To impress Marcus. His father. To show the world that she was his.

'You didn't like it?'

'It was beautiful—but...'

But she had felt as if she had been swept off her feet by a raging tsunami, going under for the third time until she couldn't see, couldn't hear, couldn't breathe. The ground had been swept from beneath her feet, and everything was running away from her. She felt the same all over again now, but for very different reasons.

'But I wanted some say in what I wore. Surely you understand that it's every girl's dream to pick out her own wedding dress.'

'I see,' he said but the look he turned on her said that he saw but he didn't understand why she would have chosen such a plain, simple design when she could have had the services of the couturier he had hired for her. 'But I would have paid...'

'And that's exactly why I didn't want it.' Alyse pulled herself up on the pillows, wishing there were fewer shadows in the room so that she could read his face more easily. 'You have already given us so much; I couldn't take any more from you.'

'It was your wedding day. I would have been happy to give you whatever you asked.'

'And you can't see that it's that *asking* that makes all the difference?'

Dario frowned darkly, trying to make sense out of something that turned everything he'd believed about her on its head and left him feeling as if the ground beneath him had suddenly shifted.

'I wanted you to have whatever you longed for—the wedding of your dreams.'

He'd wanted it to be that way for the wedding at least. When their marriage was never going to be a love match, then he could make it the sort of day she would have wanted. He couldn't do anything about the emotions.

'Or perhaps the real truth is that really you were planning on doing just what *you* wanted.'

The sudden tartness in her soft voice brought his head round sharply. She lay propped up against the pillows, her blonde hair tumbling in wild disorder around a face that had suddenly tightened unexpectedly.

'You weren't really thinking about me.'

'Why the hell would I give a damn what my bride

wears—especially when we both know that this isn't a marriage of love but one of convenience—purely a business deal?'

She clamped her lips tight shut then turned and stared out over the horizon, blinking hard in the glow of the rising sun.

'Because you wanted to rub dirt in Marcus's face to show him what he'd lost. And because you wanted your father to see what you were getting.'

There should be a thought in his head in response to that. But the truth was that there wasn't one. Just a blank space on which was etched the disturbing question—was she right? Had he really wanted her to wear something more expensive, to have all the flowers and the bridesmaids' dresses and the decorations imaginable—because that was his way of showing his father and his half-brother?

Well, if he had then it had all come back in his face to bite him. In spite of receiving an invitation, Henry Kavanaugh hadn't even shown up at the wedding. He'd sent a letter of congratulation—well, it was supposed to have been congratulations but it came with a sting in its tail that had been impossible to ignore. He could have his father's recognition at last—but at what a cost! It was a good job that this marriage had at least given Alyse what she had wanted from it—her parents' security—because it sure as hell hadn't given him any such thing.

'I thought all women had their dream weddings planned from the moment they could choose their first dress. That any woman had it all thought out—every last detail—and all they needed was the groom.'

'Any woman, hmm—?'

She turned to face him now, her neat chin coming up, openly defying him, as her green eyes flashed a challenge.

'Any woman?' she echoed cynically. 'So is that how

you see me—as just *any* woman? Any woman who would do in your bed.'

'Hell, no!'

Fury pushed him to deny it. Fury at the accusation and a rush of something darkly uncomfortable that he didn't actually want to look right in the face.

'You could never be just any woman. Do you think I would go through all this—that I would sell out my freedom and invest so much money in your family just to win *any* woman?'

He had had to mention the money, Alyse told herself. *Thanks a bunch, Dario!* If there was a way of making her feel low and cheap—correction: low and too *expensive*—then it was that. And he had sold out his freedom, had he? What the blazes did he think that she'd done? Why did he think she was here? Because she had wanted the money?

But of course that was how it would seem to him.

And, face it, Alyse, that was such a big part of it. No—she couldn't allow herself to think that. It hadn't been the money that had been the final weight in the scales as she'd tried to decide what to do. It had been because of Dario himself. Because she had wanted to be with him, under any circumstances.

'Besides, I was caught in a dilemma,' she said hastily, needing to distract him. 'You were offering one thing and my mother wanted me to wear *her* wedding dress.'

'Your mother wore that dress you had on at the wedding?'

He'd seen straight through the story she'd been about to tell.

'Well, no—but in the end I chose not to wear hers.'

'Any particular reason?' he tossed at her with apparent casualness, but she shivered at the thought of just what lay below the careless question.

The truth was she hadn't been able to bear to think of her mother's dress, handed down from one generation to another, as a symbol of her parents' love for each other. Once it had been what she'd dreamed of but now she saw how dangerous that obsessive love, one that left no room for anyone else, could be. It was that love that had got them into this mess after all. She hadn't wanted to wear anything that tied her to her parents for this wedding that, while it might be only about business and money, was also about passion and a way of breaking free from the life she had known.

'I wanted to save that for—for a proper wedding.'

'Proper?' He pounced on the word like a tiger on its prey. 'Define *proper*. Because I'm sure you don't mean it has to be oh, so correct and following every rule of polite etiquette?'

The way he pronounced the last word was so careful, so almost correct but not quite, that it tugged at her heart to think that for the first time his near perfect command of the English language had actually deserted him. It made him sound disturbingly vulnerable—but there was no way she could let herself believe that that was in fact the case.

'One that means something…something more than…'

Oh, dear, she was digging a hole right at her own feet and with every word it just got deeper.

'Something more than…?' Dario echoed ominously.

'Oh, you know what I mean, Dario. This isn't real. It isn't a genuine marriage—it's a business deal—one where you buy and I…'

'You do what? Sell yourself?' Could his voice get any more dangerous?

'Well, we both know there isn't any real feeling on either side—other than a raging burning need to get into each other's pants, of course.'

'Of course,' he echoed, clipped and icy. 'And did you explain this to your mother?'

Alyse flinched away from the ice in his words as it suddenly drained all the warmth from the sun.

'Of course not. Do you think she'd have been able to watch me walk up the aisle as a bought bride? She would have gone into a state of total collapse if she'd known that this union paid for all the ruinous mistakes she and my father had made. I just told her what I've told you—which was that I wanted to choose—and pay for—my own dress.'

This was her marriage, her wedding, her choice.

'Not every daughter wants to wear her mother's dress. Most women want their own special clothes for a special day.'

'Not my mother.' It was a flat, emotionless statement. 'She never had a wedding—never mind a dress.'

He'd touched on this once before but had made it obvious that he didn't welcome her interest in his past. But perhaps now he would let her probe a little further? It would distract him from the dangerous path his thoughts had been on, and besides she really wanted to know.

'Your father never acknowledged her?'

She might have wanted to free herself from the complications and lies her parents had told recently, but at least she had always known she was their daughter, and they had never left her in any doubt of the fact that she had been wanted, even if as a further proof of their love for each other.

'Neither her nor me. She didn't know he was married and he didn't trouble to tell her. She was supposed to have been a one-night stand and then to forget about him as he forgot about her. But then she found that she was pregnant.'

'Did she tell him?'

The way that his hands raked through the tousled blackness of his hair gave away more than he was prepared to reveal in his voice.

'Of course she did—or tried to. She wrote—she even found out his home address and saved up all she could afford to travel to his door. He wouldn't even see her. The door was shut in her face.'

Alyse's nails dug into her palms as she tried to imagine how the poor woman had felt.

'She tried again—when I was born. She took me with her and was so sure that my *father...*' he made the word sound like poison '...couldn't turn away his own son.'

There was a long pause while Dario stared out at the rising sun with narrowed eyes.

'He could. She didn't get over the doorstep and one of the servants was sent to tell her to go away or the police would be called. But she didn't give up. She tried again on my first birthday and again every year after that. She never gave up until she became ill with cancer. That year I went. I had to ask him to help her.'

How could eight simple words be filled with so much bitterness, so much emotion held back and yet clear in the sound of his voice? He had hated going but he had done so for his mother.

'I knew she had loved him in spite of everything and she would die happy if she could just see him. Or if he could do something to help ease her pain.'

'And did he?'

A brusque shake of Dario's dark head gave her the answer she was expecting.

'Not a word, not a sign. Mamma died feeling totally abandoned. But in the end it turned out that my father had never got the message. That he hadn't been in the house when I called. It was only later that I found out why.'

'Marcus?' Alyse questioned and saw again that single sharp nod that signified agreement.

It was as if the sun had suddenly gone behind a deep dark cloud, taking all the warmth from the air. The rivalry and hatred between the two brothers had deep roots and a long time to grow.

'I swore I'd never have anything to do with them ever again.'

'So how did you know about my mother's gambling—my dad's problems?'

Dario's smile was a travesty of any sort of amusement.

'I didn't want anything to do with the Kavanaughs but I have contacts—it's easy to get information if I want it. That was how I learned that Henry had had a stroke and that now Marcus was in charge.'

And he had wanted his revenge on Marcus for the way the older brother had denied Dario's dying mother the chance of any peace of mind.

'From there it was an easy job to discover that my damned brother was making a play for you—and why. You were just the sort of trophy wife that would be the icing on Kavanaugh's cake and, best of all, you could be manoeuvred into accepting his proposal when it was either that or see your family destroyed.'

'And that was why you came looking for me from the start?'

He didn't trouble to deny it but he didn't show any sort of concern at her accusation. But it damaged something inside her when she knew he'd moved straight onto the attack, to get his revenge on his brother, the way his father had rejected him and his mother.

Her thoughts were reeling back to that first evening she'd met him, on the night of the ball. He'd come straight across the room to her and she'd thought it was because he couldn't help himself—that he'd been so attracted to her. But then there had been that moment when she'd introduced herself and just for a second he had reacted unexpectedly. She had barely noticed it at the time but now she could hear his voice saying her name and something in the intonation of it caught on her nerves.

'You introduced yourself to me—remember. I had my suspicions but then you confirmed them.'

'So is that what I am to you too...' her voice cracked on the question '...a trophy wife?'

Dario twisted in the bed so that he was looking down into her face.

'You're the only wife I'd ever want. I told you, I don't do family.'

Which was like giving her something and snatching it right back with the second breath. Was she still just a pawn in his game to outwit and take retribution on his callous family?

'If it helps,' Dario said slowly, something in the way he looked at her telling her that he had read her thoughts in her face, 'I never expected to want you as much as I did from the moment I saw you.'

'So it wasn't just to get at Marcus—and your father?'

She was ridiculously pleased to know that at least.

'Never just that. There was something there between us like an electrical storm in the moment we met. And you felt it too—don't deny it.'

'I'm not denying it.' Alyse looked deep into his eyes as she spoke, wanting him to know it was true. 'I can't.'

'It was inevitable—it would have happened once we met, no matter who you were, no matter who I was.'

His hand was on her as he spoke, strong fingers moving up her arm, over her shoulders. At first the softness of his touch made her shiver as the nerves beneath her skin began to tingle in instinctive response. Another moment and her pulse had set up a slow, heavy thud that made the blood pound inside her head.

'Inevitable...' she murmured, her eyes half closing as she gave herself up to the pleasure of his caress.

'Totally...' Dario's voice was low, the sound of it like warm smoke coiling around her. His hand was moving down her body, so slowly, so gently, and this time when she shivered it was in a rush of newly awakened need, the tiny moan that escaped her impossible to hold back as she shifted restlessly against the soft white sheets.

'Totally inevitable,' she sighed again as he pulled her underneath him and proceeded to take her senses by storm until she was totally incapable of saying or thinking of anything else but him and the glorious sensual power of his body taking possession of hers.

CHAPTER NINE

'*BUONGIORNO*, SLEEPING BEAUTY...'

Dario dropped a kiss on Alyse's smiling mouth as she yawned and stretched, slowly coming awake.

'Are you ever going to wake up today?'

'Mmm?' she murmured, stirring slightly and then curling up under the covers in the way he had come to love. She looked like a small, delicate kitten twisting herself into a ball and his fingers itched to stroke down the clear line of her spine, watch her arch into the caress, press herself against his palm.

'Are you going to get up?'

'Wake up, maybe...'

She turned a slow, sleepy smile on him, one that twisted his guts into knots of hunger, made his body harden in an instant.

'But I didn't plan on getting up at all today. In fact, I planned on staying right where I am but...I thought you might want to join me.'

Reaching out, she aimed for his hands, but then brushed against his leg, frowning as her fingers felt the linen of his trousers.

'Oh, but this won't do—won't do at all.'

She pursed her mouth into a moue of sulky provocation.

'You have to take these off—and everything else.'

'Alyse!'

He blended reproach with amusement in order to hide just how much he wanted to do exactly as she said. At least with her eyes still half-closed she couldn't see the hard and hungry evidence of his body that gave away the fact that he was just pretending to object to what she was saying.

'Dario!' She mocked his tone perfectly. 'I don't know why you're objecting—I think we should spend all day in bed. Eat a little—perhaps drink some wine but only in between—when we need refreshment. The rest of the time, I think we should make love again and again and again.'

She writhed sensually as she spoke, adding further discomfort to his hardened state as the movement brought her naked body clear of any covers, the shafts of sunlight slipping through the gauze at the windows highlighting the creamy skin of her breasts, the pert pink tips of her nipples that made his mouth water to remember the way they tasted.

'But we did that yesterday—and the day before...'

'And can you think of any better way of spending our time?'

Her eyes came wide open, gleaming emerald in the sun as she stared at him.

'Or have you tired of me? Is that it?'

'Tired of you?' His laughter was shaken as the way she sat up made her breasts sway softly. 'Hell, woman, do you really think that's possible?'

But the faint frown that drew her brows together bothered him. It looked as if there was something that was troubling her—but what? She had been warm and passionate, giving and hungry for pleasure all through the night, as she had been for so many nights since they had arrived at the villa. He had found her totally insatiable, impossible to resist. In fact there had been that one time, the first morning, that they had both been so turned on that he had forgotten his never-without-a-condom rule. If it hadn't been for the fact that she was on the Pill...

He snatched his mind back from the erotic path it was following and made himself look deep into her questioning eyes.

'How could I be tired of you? Did I seem tired last night...well...' this time his laughter was more natural, rather self-deprecating as he recalled the way they had finally fallen into exhausted sleep, unable to keep awake any longer '...except for once.'

That shadowed look was still there so he put his thoughts back onto the track of distracting her—and going on with the plan he had come in here to suggest.

'I thought we could go out for the day. You should see something of Italy.'

'Go where? What's near here?'

'Well, there's Bologna or Florence—Pisa. Oh, no.' It was a light-hearted groan as he saw the new light of interest in her eyes. 'You want to do the tourist thing? See the Leaning Tower?'

'I can think of another leaning tower I'd rather see...'

The direction of her stare, the wicked curve to her mouth made it plain exactly what she meant.

'But if that's not on offer—then Pisa it has to be. Is that close to the Campo Santo as well?'

'Within walking distance. Why?'

Something of that teasing look had gone from her face.

'I was told there were some frescoes there that are worth seeing. Oh, don't look like that!' she added as she caught the fleeting expression of disbelief that flashed across his face. 'I did study the History of Art at university.'

He'd always assumed that she had taken the unchallenging job because she was comfortable coasting, enjoying her parents' comfortable lifestyle. But he was learning he had been so wrong about so much.

'You did? Then why the hell…?'

'Was I just working as a receptionist?' She supplied the end of the question for him. 'At least I was working in the art world—but my mother was so often ill and she needed someone close to look after her. That's why I still lived at home. But don't worry…' she hurried to say it in order to get rid of the dark clouds that had come rushing over his face '…that's not going to be the way it is any more. For one thing—I'm not going back to the gallery. I gave in my notice as soon as we…as we came to our arrangement. And for another…'

'How long has your mother been ill?'

'She's had the mood swings as long as I can remember.' Alyse's mouth twisted into a grimace of distaste. 'I grew up knowing I had to be careful—not upset her any further.'

Her mother couldn't help the emotional seesaw she lived on, she knew, but, looking back, she could see how her father had indulged his wife, always tiptoeing around her 'delicate sensitivity', always caring for her—or asking their daughter to do so—in a way that made sure she never truly faced up to the repercussions of her actions. Until this final terrible mess that they would never have got out of if it hadn't been for Dario.

'You've done quite enough for her,' Dario put in roughly, and she nodded slowly in agreement.

'It's up to my father now,' Alyse agreed sombrely, knowing once again that amazing sense of freedom that she had woken up with every morning since Dario had made his proposal about their marriage. It was only now, since she had come to Italy with him, that she had got rid of that sense of being used, of being a pawn in her parents' lives rather than free to live for herself. It was weird that even when she was tied by the pre-nup that she had signed she'd felt more liberated and more alive than ever before. 'I can't live my mother's life for her. I can only live my own.'

'So—the frescoes.'

'And all the rest of it—the Leaning Tower—the whole tourist bit.'

Alyse felt her mouth curve into a smile, her mood lightening as she tossed back the covers, pushed herself to her feet. 'Just give me half an hour to get ready...Dario?'

Seeing how his eyes were focused on her naked body, she smiled then wagged a pretend reproving finger at him. 'No! You promised me a day out.'

'A day out...' Dario managed, his throat dry with desire. 'And then we go back to bed.'

Back to bed...Alyse thought much later that day, as she tossed and turned in the huge bed, trying to find somewhere comfortable to rest her throbbing head. She doubted that Dario had had *this* in mind when he had planned on getting her back into his bed.

But the headache that had threatened on the journey from the Villa D'Oro had turned into a full-blooded migraine by the time they had seen the frescoes and, knowing what was coming, she could only beg Dario that they head back immediately. They'd just made it before the sickness began and she had been completely out of things for the next twenty-four hours.

She wouldn't have blamed Dario if he had dumped her on his staff and left, but she couldn't have been more mistaken. From the moment they'd arrived back at the villa, he had lifted her off her feet and carried her carefully upstairs to the bedroom. There he had undressed her with gentle hands, so very different from the heated way they had torn at each other's clothes only the night before. He'd laid her down on cool, smooth sheets, brought the medication she needed and, much to her embarrassment, the bowl that had soon become vitally important.

The rest of the time had been something of an unpleasant haze. The one thing she had known was that if she needed him Dario was there, his voice soft in her ears, his hand cool on her head. He wiped her horrible sweaty face with a damp cloth and fed her sips of water when she could manage to keep them down.

At last, after the usual forty-eight hours, she had felt the nightmare receding and, having slept through the second night, she eventually felt well enough to get to her feet. Changing out of her crumpled nightgown and pulling on a white cotton robe, she made her way downstairs to find Dario sitting on the terrace, a mug of coffee in his hands, staring out at the green and gold landscape across the valley where the dawn was just beginning to break, gilding the mellow brickwork of the villa in its light.

'*Buongiorno, mio marito...*' she said, startling him so that he looked round sharply, obviously dragging himself back from wherever his thoughts had taken him.

'*Buongiorno, mia moglie.*'

Impossibly, considering the fact that it was his native language, he seemed to be the one struggling with the use of Italian. Or perhaps it was the fact that she had called him 'husband' that he was having a problem with.

'Should you be out of bed?'

He was on his feet, bringing a chair closer, plumping up cushions for her.

'I'm fine, Dario. It's usually all over and done with in a couple of days. It just looks awful while it's happening.'

But she sat down rather hastily anyway. She might be feeling better but she wasn't quite ready for the sight of Dario, shirtless and barefoot, in only a pair of long shorts riding low on his narrow hips.

'But I'd love something to drink—is that lemonade?'

'Naturalmente.'

He poured her a glass of the cool, cloudy liquid, ice chinking against the sides as he passed it to her. Alyse drank with relish, thankful to have something to ease the tightness in her throat. There was something very different about Dario this morning, but she couldn't put her finger on just what.

'Does that happen often?'

'Luckily, no.' Alyse focused her gaze on the rising sun over on the horizon so that she didn't have to meet his eyes as she remembered the way she'd been the previous morning. 'I'm sorry...'

That made his dark eyebrows snap together sharply in a frown. 'Sorry—what for?'

'Well—you didn't exactly sign on for the role of nurse.'

He'd wanted a lover, someone attractive and desirable in his bed. She hadn't felt at all desirable over the past couple of days, and she didn't know where he'd slept but it hadn't been in the same bed as her. She had a vague memory of waking once or twice and he had always been in a chair near to her bed, his long body sprawled uncomfortably, head resting against one hand as he watched her.

'For better, for worse. In sickness and in health,' Dario quoted sardonically.

Those vows belonged to a real marriage. She didn't want to think about the rest of them, the way that it went on to the line 'Till death us do part'. That was a vow that was never going to be met in this marriage. It was shocking how much that hurt.

'How long is this marriage supposed to last for?'

She was horrified by the way the words slipped past her unguarded lips. How could she have spoken her thoughts out loud—and, even worse, without a trace of the uncertainty she really felt about it? Instead, she sounded impatient and demanding and obviously Dario thought so too as his frown darkened ominously.

'You're already tiring of things?'

'N-no.' Alyse gulped down a hasty swallow of lemonade in an attempt to ease the way her throat seemed to have closed up. 'I mean…who could ever tire of living here…?'

Her rather wild gesture took in the sweep of the valley before them, the sparkling blue of the swimming pool off to the right, the long, winding drive down to the road.

'It's heaven but…'

But not her heaven. Not the sort of paradise she should get to love too much because one day it was going to be snatched away from her. In just the way that, at some point in the future, Dario too would leave.

Awkwardly she choked on her drink as she realised just where her thoughts were headed. She had thought of Dario and *love* in the same moment, dreading and regretting the fact that he would be snatched away from her when he tired of this pretend marriage. Probably all too soon. After all, the last couple of days could not have been the fantasy non-stop sexual orgy he had hoped for.

'Why did you bring me here?' she asked, not daring to go too close to the thoughts that were inside her head.

'You know why.'

'You wanted to do things properly.'

Suddenly the refreshingly tart taste of the lemonade had turned to bitter acid. She had known the 'honeymoon' image of their trip to Tuscany had been just that—a pretence to make everything seem real—and she'd been all right with that at the beginning. But things had changed so much in the past three weeks that it was all so totally different now and she was only just beginning to see how that had happened in such a short space of time.

'And I wanted you to see my home.'

My home, not *our* home. *Oh, come on, Alyse! You knew it was that from the start—when you first arrived here. So why should it matter so much more now?*

Because at the start she had felt so very differently. Because in the beginning she had been so grateful to Dario for what he had done, and that wonderful sense of freedom had made her head spin with the joy of it. She had been hugely attracted to him, had wanted him passionately...but she had never felt like this. Never felt that it would break her heart when the time came to leave Villa D'Oro—and him.

Because—somewhere along the road since their fake engagement, their marriage of business deals and sexual need—she had fallen crazily in love with her husband of convenience. The thought was so disturbing, so dangerous that she wanted to think of anything but that.

'Did...did your mother ever live here?' she asked for something to say, needing to distract herself—to distract him from the sudden thickness in her throat, the unexpected rough edge to her voice.

'Not live here, no.'

Dario's voice hitched on the last sentence. He had never been able to help his mother when she was ill. He hadn't earned enough to give her the comfort he had longed to find for her, but at least he could find a way to remember her.

'I bought the villa in my mother's memory. She had always loved it when she was alive, and once confided that her dream would be to make a home in such a place.'

'It's a magical place.'

Dario could only nod, privately acknowledging that the Villa D'Oro had worked some sort of magic on him since he'd arrived here this time. He'd been living the past weeks in a self-indulgent, indolent haze, content to spend his days showing Alyse the beauties of Tuscany, and at night rediscovering the beauties of her body. They had indulged themselves in other ways too, eating good food and drinking the best wines his vineyards produced. It had been a long, lazy, hedonistic existence—the sort of holiday that he never took—and no one would ever believe he could have been so idle for so long. He'd never wanted to before.

I wanted you to see my home, he'd said and now he realised he'd never said that to anyone ever before. Not to any other woman. In fact he'd never brought a woman here.

And yet he'd stayed here for several weeks now, off duty in a way he'd never been before. A couple of days in the Villa D'Oro and he was usually itching to get back to work. But not this time. Something had changed this time. Alyse had changed things.

'I wish my mother could have seen this place, just once. Seen her dream.'

But that was another thing that Alyse had changed. He knew that in his mother's mind, her dream would have included him with a wife—a real wife. He couldn't stay and pretend that he had a marriage. It felt wrong when the union was just an illusion, even if he was acknowledging his mother's other dream—that of seeing him united with his father.

'And I wish she could see you now,' Alyse put in softly. Just the sound of her voice tugged on something sharply inside him, making him stare into the sun so intently that he almost felt it would sear the sight from his eyes. Or any shadow of his so-called family from his mind. But it would take more than that to erase those unwelcome thoughts. The ones he had thought he wanted and now could only feel as a weight on his shoulders, a dark shadow that lay over even a day as beautiful as this one.

'I invited my father to the wedding,' he said suddenly, seeing Alyse's start of surprise at the abrupt change of subject. 'He didn't turn up.'

That hadn't been unexpected, Alyse knew, though she couldn't forget the way he'd been looking around as they'd walked down the aisle—looking for someone. In spite of his cynically nonchalant approach, had he actually hoped that his father might turn up when his rejected illegitimate son had married that 'trophy wife' Marcus had failed to win?

I don't do family. It was no wonder that Dario had tossed out that cold-blooded declaration. He had never had a family to learn how to exist with.

'He's a fool,' she said earnestly. 'An idiot not to want to connect with a son that any other man would be proud of.'

'You think?' He shot her a sideways, darkly sceptical glance, one that had shadows in it that were nothing to do with the effects of the sun on the horizon.

'But of course—you've dragged yourself up by your bootstraps from very difficult beginnings. You've made a fortune for yourself, unlike Marcus, who had all the privileges and education from the start.'

'I thought that way once,' Dario stated flatly. 'All the money I made—each thousand then eventually each million—I let myself believe that this time he had to notice me. When I matched him euro for euro—when I outstripped him...'

His bark of laughter was so bleak, so raw, so totally without any touch of humour that it made Alyse wince back into her chair, blinking hard to force away the burn of tears at the back of her eyes.

'You'd have thought I'd have got used to the silence by now.'

'Like I said, your father's a fool. You're the son who

proved himself—not just the son who inherited everything.'

That made Dario twist in his seat so that he was looking directly at her, his dark head blotting out the sun. He
could see her perfectly, but his face was just a black silhouette against the rising glow.

'And what about the son who had to blackmail a wife
into his bed?'

She hated the way he asked that. Hated the black thread
of cynicism that ran through the words.

'You didn't do that! You didn't *blackmail* me. I was
willing—so willing.'

When he lifted one black brow in mocking question she
was up and out of her chair in a moment.

Moving across the terrace, she bent down and kissed
him on the mouth, long and slow. The white robe and the
neck of her nightgown gaped as she did so and she saw
from the way his eyes darkened that he was clearly well
aware of it.

'I was willing…' she repeated, sliding onto his lap, feeling the pressure of his erection, hot under the cotton of his
shorts, against her body as she straddled him. 'I still am.'

'Alyse…' His hands came up to hold her, burying themselves in the fall of her hair as she increased the pressure
of her lips against his partly open mouth.

'Let me show you how willing I am.'

With her hands between them, she tugged down the
zip of his shorts, freeing him so that his powerful shaft
came up against the moistness of her where she sat above
him. It took only a moment or two's adjustment, taking
him firmly in her hand to position him just right before
she sank down onto him, hearing his groan of dark satisfaction as she took him into her.

'Does this look like blackmail to you?' she muttered thickly as the hunger took hold of her. 'Does it?'

But Dario was beyond speech and he could only shake his dark head in response to the question as Alyse began to move, sliding up and down with deliberate pressure. He held still for a few intense moments until he gave a moan of surrender, reached out and dragged her closer, pulling her head down to his, crushing her mouth with his as he abandoned himself to her.

CHAPTER TEN

DARIO READ THE email message over again, cursing under his breath as he did so.

How the hell had time got away from him so badly? It never had before.

The meeting he'd been sent a reminder about had been planned months ago. Before he'd married his convenient wife. Hell—before he'd even met Alyse. It had been the reason he was originally in London when he'd found out about Marcus's nasty little underhand scheme to blackmail Alyse into marriage.

But that had been before the night of the ball. The night he now thought of as the night of Alyse. The night that had knocked him completely off balance. And he had never been able to think quite straight since.

An example of that was the fact that he had actually forgotten this meeting. He never forgot anything. Certainly not something like this.

Cursing again, he slammed down an answer—'I'll be there'—and stabbed his finger on 'send'.

Perhaps this reminder was important in other ways too. It had prompted him to realise just what was happening—and to see what needed to be done to stop the rot. This meeting was important—he couldn't get out of it—but what really mattered was the business with his father. That had to be dealt with and sooner rather than later. Something burned in his guts at just the thought of it, but he knew there was no getting away from it.

'You should pack your bags after breakfast.'

The command came at Alyse over the table. Breakfast was usually her favourite time of day, with the sun not yet too hot, both of them still slightly sleepy and something of the intensity of the closeness of the night still lingering around them like scented smoke. But today was different; that much was obvious from the moment she'd woken to find that Dario was no longer in the bed beside her. He had already been up and dressed and it was as if the unexpectedly formal rich blue shirt and black trousers were like a coat of armour, closing him off from their normal regular routine.

'Oh?' She paused with a spoonful of yoghurt halfway to her mouth. 'Why?'

'We're going back to England.'

Dario's focus was on his tablet computer, a faint frown drawing his brows together as he read through opened emails. He'd never done that before either, and it made her shift uncomfortably in her seat.

'Just like that?'

She didn't trouble to iron the unease from her voice and at least it earned her a pause in his focus, the blue eyes flicking up sharply to fix on her face.

'I have business to attend to.'

Which was perfectly reasonable, so why did it make her feel so troubled? She had known that their idyll at the Villa D'Oro couldn't last for ever; in fact she'd been waiting for Dario to decree that their 'honeymoon' was over. So why did her stomach feel as if a thousand butterflies were battering their wings frantically against the sides, looking for escape? The yoghurt didn't taste right either, she thought, hastily putting the spoon back in the bowl and reaching for a glass of water. The truth was that she wasn't at all hungry this morning. She'd felt that way for a couple of days but, mixed in with the upset of Dario's announcement, it felt worse today.

'OK, then, I'll get on to it.'

'Do that. The car will be here at ten.'

So soon? He had woken up this morning and decreed that it was time to get back to work and that was it. No explanations—just a snap of the fingers and she had to obey. The tiny bit of yoghurt she had eaten seemed to curdle in her stomach, all pleasure in her food ruined.

The sight of the smoothly made, fresh-sheeted bed that greeted her as she went into their bedroom seemed to symbolise all that had just happened downstairs, making her sigh in despondency. When she had woken the covers had been in the wild tangle they had created last night. Several pillows had been on the floor, the one that Dario had used in the night and that still smelled of his hair and skin tucked underneath her cheek, where she had tugged it when he'd eased himself out of the bed. Now all that wonderfully sensual jumble had been smoothed away. The bed looked pristine and immaculate, as if nothing so wild as uninhibited lovemaking had ever darkened its sheets.

Lovemaking...

Alyse tugged open a drawer and started pulling out a bundle of her underwear. Why call it *love*making when the truth was that to Dario it was simply sex that he had paid for? As in that damned pre-nup she had signed.

But... Alyse's head came up sharply as she tried to remember just what else had been in that contract. She couldn't properly recall...and the sudden movement had made her head swim so badly that she had to sit down rather rapidly on the bed rather than fall to the floor.

She didn't want to get on with the packing, she admitted to herself. She wanted to stay because here at least she was in Dario's home. Here, they had the illusion of a marriage. If they went back to London then things would change. Dario would no longer be the man he was in the sunlit warmth of Tuscany. He would focus on his work and she would be installed in that huge apartment, a kept woman. And the worst thing of all was that she would have to try to convince everyone that she was blissfully happy—deeply in love with Dario and he with her.

Well, the first would be easy enough—but, even if Dario played his part well, she'd know he just didn't mean it.

She didn't want this to end and she was afraid that returning to London would do just that—end it. It seemed inevitable that, once this 'honeymoon' was over, reality would set in. Reality and the prospect of facing up to what she had really done in marrying Dario—and, even worse, giving her heart to him.

He'd provided the pre-nup because she had demanded it, and he had kept his word on the way he had helped her parents out of the monstrous hole they had dug themselves into. But he hadn't explained any further details, made it clear just why he thought this marriage was worth it to him. Other than thwarting the half-brother he detested. She'd thought that he might set a period to the length of their marriage and had been frankly surprised that he hadn't done any such thing.

I offered marriage—not commitment and devotion for life.

His words came back to haunt her. This wasn't a real marriage, so inevitably it must end at some point—but when? How long would Dario want to keep her with him, in his bed, in his life? Until he tired of her. But how would she know when he did? And how would she cope when he discarded her?

While they'd been here at the Villa D'Oro, she'd been able to enjoy his company, share his bed, had been the focus of his attention and, loving him as she did, she had revelled in it. But what would she do when he told her it was over? How would she handle seeing him with someone else? She felt nausea rise in her throat at the thought.

'Enough!' she told herself sharply. She'd been told to pack, and Dario would certainly scent a rat if he came in and found her sitting on her bed, staring at the floor. He'd want to know what was up, and she couldn't possibly tell him. Pushing back the queasiness that still bothered her, she got to her feet and turned towards the wardrobe. The prospect of flying while she felt like this only added to her discomfort.

The flight to England, short though it was, turned into a journey from hell. From the moment they took off until Dario's jet landed in London it was a battle to keep the sickness she was feeling from showing. To make matters worse, she now had to deal with a growing suspicion that there could be a disturbing, shocking explanation behind the way she was feeling. One that seemed to drain all the strength from her body and kept her silent and still until they reached his apartment at last.

'I'm going to have to go out again... Sorry, but it can't be helped.'

That 'sorry' would sound more convincing if he wasn't already halfway to the door, but Alyse was actually relieved to see him go.

Using the excuse of needing painkillers—praying Dario would take her withdrawal as being caused by the arrival of her period—a period she had now worked out was in fact well overdue—she had managed a diversion into a chemist's and had snatched up a vital testing kit, pushing it to the bottom of her bag, where she now felt as if it was close to burning a hole in the leather.

'No problem. I understand.' Her reply was vague, off-hand, her attention elsewhere.

The door had barely slammed shut behind him before she turned and headed for the bathroom, pulling the pregnancy testing kit out of its packaging with shaking hands. She had to know.

I don't do family.

Oh, heaven, why did she have to remember that line, and the absolute conviction with which it was spoken, right now?

She knew Dario didn't 'do family' and who could blame him after the way his father and his horrible half-brother had behaved? How could a man who had grown up unwanted by his father, disowned and ignored, and then pushed away as the result of Marcus's scheming, ever want to 'do family'? The ghastly old man hadn't even bothered to come to the wedding, after Dario had made the effort to ask.

What was the time she was supposed to wait for this thing to develop? Three minutes?

How was she supposed to stand still and watch it for three minutes…? It was an eternity—dragging out unbearably.

Clutching the white stick in her hand, Alyse paced round the bathroom and then, when that was not enough, into the living room. Desperate to distract herself from the waiting, the ticking by of seconds that seemed to last for ever, she tried opening cupboards, pulling out drawers. It was an aimless exercise, simply filling in time, but…

'Oh…'

Shock blurred her eyes, and she let the test stick drop

from her hand into the last drawer she'd opened, then hastily snatched it up again, her eyes fixed not on it but the papers it had landed on.

'No...'

The headed notepaper was an immediate giveaway, the Kavanaugh name emblazoned across the top. *Henry* Kavanaugh's name. The letters danced before her eyes as she grabbed at the papers, crumpling them in a shaking hand.

Why had Dario's father written to the son he had discarded and abandoned, and then scorned when Dario had tried to make contact, to break down the barriers between them? There were actually two letters, but right now she couldn't get past the first one because when she focused on it the date it had been written struck her like a blow to her chest, taking away every trace of breath.

This letter had been written before their wedding. Before Dario had paid off her father's debts. Before even he had come to her to suggest their business deal marriage, with her as the convenient bride. But how convenient she had never even begun to guess. She had thought that Dario had offered the marriage as a way of helping her parents because he had wanted her so much. Because she had been enough for him. Now she was slapped in the face by the fact that there had been something he had wanted so much more—something she could never give him but that he could use her to get for himself.

She'd thought that with Dario she had found herself, and her freedom at last, but she had been used, deceived, betrayed from start to finish. And this was the cruellest deceit of all. The worst lie.

The last lie, she vowed silently as the letter slipped from her weakened grasp, falling back into the drawer in the same moment that Alyse remembered the test stick that she still held in her hand. The three minutes were well and truly up.

'Oh, no.'

Her head spun wildly, sickeningly, as she looked down at the window where the result was displayed only too clearly and with no room for mistake.

Pregnant.

Pregnant.

'Oh, no, oh, no…no, no!'

'Oh, no—*what*?'

She hadn't heard the footsteps or the door open behind her but there was no mistaking just who had come into the room. She didn't even need to turn round to see. There was no mistaking Dario's presence, Dario's voice.

'I couldn't leave—I knew something was up. So what is it? Just what the hell is going on here?'

CHAPTER ELEVEN

'I'M PREGNANT.'

Alyse couldn't think of any other way to answer him. And really, why hedge about it, or try to sugar-coat things? There was no easy way to say it. She might have wished for a little time to catch her breath, to get used to the idea herself, but now that Dario was here there was no point in trying to do anything but tell him the truth. And the reality was that she wanted the truth to be told. From now on, nothing but the truth.

'I'm pregnant...' she said again in a very different tone, an irrepressible, overwhelming note of awe creeping into the words.

The only response was total silence from behind her but she didn't dare to turn round to see what sort of expression went along with that total stillness. She just wished he would speak—say something, anything so that she could know what she was dealing with, understand a little of what he was thinking.

She heard Dario draw in a rough, ragged breath and let it out again. He was still giving nothing away.

'You're sure?' he said at last and that had her spinning on her heel, whirling round to face him whether she was ready or not.

'Of course I'm sure! I can read.'

She waved the white stick wildly in the air then pushed it towards him so that he could see it for himself.

'Pregnant. That's what that word says. *Pregnant*. With child. Expecting. I'm having your baby, Dario…and if you say "How?" then I'll…'

'I'm not going to.' Dario's tone was flat, emotionless. 'I'm only too well aware of just *how* you became pregnant. But when—the night before you had the migraine?'

'Or after it…the time on the terrace.' It was ridiculous to blush at the memory but she still felt the fiery colour rush into her cheeks. 'I was so sick that I hadn't taken my pill for a couple of days.'

When she'd seduced him out there in the sunlight without a thought for the possible consequences. Consequences that had now become all too real.

It was the last thing he'd considered when he'd realised something was up, Dario acknowledged to himself. He was all sorts of a fool because it should have been one of the first thoughts that had come to mind, but the truth was that he hadn't even considered it. They had used contraception every time but two. And, in spite of those two slip-ups, he had known that she was on the Pill.

He'd damned well forgotten how sick she had been. No tablet could have stayed in her stomach after the onslaught of those two days. So there was little doubt exactly when this had happened—or even where.

The only question was what they did about it.

For the moment his mind wouldn't move on to answering that question. All he could think of was the fact that Alyse was pregnant with his child. His eyes went to the flat plane of her stomach, the curve of her hips in the tight denim jeans she had worn to travel in. There was no sign, no swell of a baby bump. But how could there be? It was still so early…

How could something so totally invisible have such an impact that it left him feeling as if someone had punched him on the jaw, stunning his brain?

He was going to be a father.

'That was very special…'

He could see that he'd stunned her in turn. The lush pink mouth that had opened to say something else now stayed slightly open, bemused and silent. Did she really not think he'd spoken the truth? How could she doubt it when his body had hardened and ached from just the memory?

'But I know…' She was struggling to speak firmly, making him frown. 'I know you don't…'

I don't do family. Oh, he'd been so sure when he'd said that, burning up with conviction. And he still wouldn't cross the road to any member of his living family. His so-called father had made sure of that. But a family he'd never met. *Dio mio*, a family he'd made—they'd made between them? He'd never thought it would ever be a possibility, had made damn sure that it was never likely to be, and so he hadn't prepared himself for how he would react if it happened.

I don't do family.

He was going to be a *father.*

But, having spent so much of his life trying to prove himself to the father he had never had, what the hell did he know about being a parent? Wasn't that something you learned by example? By watching the way your father behaved…

Hell, no! His thoughts shuddered away from the idea of ever being anything like the man who had merely been his mother's sperm donor. Because there was no way that Henry Kavanaugh merited being termed anything else.

He had nothing to compare it with. Nothing that told him what this sort of a family would be.

Where the devil was this going? He might have been the one who was most unsure about this, but Alyse sure as hell looked every bit as uncomfortable as he felt.

'I…'

He opened his mouth to answer her but he had hesitated a moment too long and already she was rushing in to fill the silence.

'But don't worry. I won't ask anything from you.'

If she'd thought to appease him, ease his anger, Alyse recognised, she couldn't have been more wrong. The burn of his glare told her that, and the world tilted around her so that she had to grab at a chair for support.

'You won't need to ask,' he declared, clipped and cold. 'I know my duty. I gave you an allowance once we were married—though I see no sign of the way you've spent it.'

Ice-blue eyes swept over her worn jeans and loose red shirt, and the thought that he considered all he'd done for her as his *duty* was more than she could bear. Would that be his attitude to this baby too? That he would consider his part in its life as his *duty*?

'Why would I need anything from you? There's nothing I can spend the money on. I mean—you gave me all those clothes, even after the wedding, more jewellery than I could possibly wear. I lived in a palace in Tuscany—and now here in a penthouse…'

Her hands waved wildly, indicating the huge room, the wide expanse of London beyond the huge plate glass windows. The frown that was his response made her legs turn to water. Had she blundered in, declaring that she considered this place her home? Was that never to be? Was this how it ended?

He'd never put a time limit on their convenient marriage, but had it really come quite this soon? But of course the news she'd hit him with went against everything he wanted from life. And, as that appalling letter in the drawer had revealed, what he wanted in life was far from *her*. Instead, she had only been a means to an end to get what he really wanted from his father—recognition and revenge.

'I had more food than I can eat—'

The bitterness of her recent discovery put more venom into her words than they merited and she watched as Dario's black brows drew together in a dark frown. Was he beginning to guess that there was something else behind all this? She wasn't going to let him off.

'What else could I need?'

What else, other than a man who really wanted to be married to her? Who *loved*…?

No! Her mind danced away from that thought. She couldn't let it in, didn't dare to let it sneak through any crack in her defensive armour and take root in her mind, in her heart.

'We had a contract.'

'We did.'

But a contract was all they had. She was the fool who'd allowed herself to consider the possibility that there might be more.

'And I meant to keep to it, but a child… A child is not in the contract,' Alyse managed, getting control over her voice only by making it sound as stiff as her lips and spine.

'To hell with the contract! Unless…'

He suddenly broke off, fixed his burning gaze on her face until she squirmed under the force of it. She pushed her chin upwards to meet that blazing blue glare, trying to hide the way her stomach was quailing inside, tying itself into agonising knots.

'You weren't planning to abort...?'

'Oh, no—no!'

He sounded furious, appalled. No wonder, when the letter she had seen made it clear that a child was an essential part of the other contract—the one he had with his devil of a father.

'But a child was definitely not part of the plan—there was nothing about it in the pre-nup.'

Because neither of them had thought that would happen. She had thought that she was protected. He had thought that she was—and they had taken that one crazy risk...

Or had they?

Dear God, but was this worse than she had thought? Had Dario deliberately 'forgotten' about contraception so that they would end up in just this situation? Her mind already felt bruised from what she had learned. Only now, slowly and unwillingly, was she beginning to face up to all that must lie behind it.

She knew that she couldn't live with it. It would tear her heart in half to leave, but it would shatter it beyond repair to stay, knowing why he had wanted her, why he had married her.

'You don't have to stay married to me—to "do the right thing"—just because I'm pregnant,' she managed through lips tight with the cold despair that gripped her. 'I can manage on my own...'

'And just how will you manage? You left your job to come to me. I will provide for the child, of course...'

Of course... He would want to be seen to be doing his duty by the baby.

'And you have your allowance.'

'Are you saying I'll still be entitled to an allowance even as your ex-wife?'

'Ex-wife?'

He made it into a sound of pure disbelief, his dark head going back as if she'd slapped him.

'This marriage isn't over. We are not separating. I will not let you go!'

It was the most brutal of ironies, Alyse acknowledged miserably, that just a few short hours ago—less—those might have been the words she most wanted to hear from him. That she would have thought she was dreaming if he had told her he wanted their marriage to continue—that he had no intention of separating from her. But now she knew exactly why he was saying that, and that knowledge turned her hope of a dream into the darkest, most bitter nightmare.

'Of course not.' She laced her response with pure acid, watched as he actually dared to frown at her tone. 'That just wouldn't do, would it? You'd never satisfy your father that way.'

'What the hell has my father...?'

'He won't pay out on an *ex*-wife and child, will he? Not when he wants a respectable marriage, a legitimate grandbaby. You have to give him everything he asks for, you know, otherwise you'll never be able to move into Kavanaugh House—the *family home*.'

He was catching on now. The mention of Kavanaugh House had done it. She saw those blue eyes look behind her, go to where the drawer she had pulled out still hung open, the letter from Henry Kavanaugh clearly seen inside it.

'The letter.'

Alyse had once been told how close the emotions of love and hate were to each other. She'd never fully believed it, but now she thought she really understood. Dario stood before her, tall, dark, stunning; the man she had fallen in love with. But he was also the man who had betrayed her. He had lied to her, used her to get what he wanted every bit as deliberately as her parents had. She hated that. She hated him for doing that to her.

'Yes, the letter. The letter your father sent you before you ever asked me to marry you. Do you remember what it says—or do I have to remind you?'

'Hell, no…'

Dario needed no reminder about what that letter said. How could he when it had burned into his mind ever since he had first read it. It was the letter that had started all this. That had made him see there was a way that he could do more than thwart Marcus in his half-brother's campaign to take Alyse as his wife and so fulfil the old man's deepest wish. Getting the family estate, and Kavanaugh House as his reward.

It was that letter that had sent him to the Gregorys' home on the day that he had discovered the financial mess Alyse's father was in. The mess that Marcus had been determined to take advantage of and force Alyse to be his bride, even though she had made it plain that that was the last thing she wanted.

The letter that had held out a tempting suggestion of a possible reconciliation, or at least an acknowledgement of who he was and the fact that Henry Kavanaugh was his father. He would even be given the family home if he, rather than his half-brother, was the one to give the old man the fulfilment of his dream. Something that his mother had dreamed of right up until the day she'd died.

'My fa—Kavanaugh wrote to tell me that he'd changed

his will. He offered me an acknowledgement of the fact that I was his son.'

'And a nice big, juicy carrot in the shape of Kavanaugh House.'

'That wasn't what I wanted.'

'No?' Alyse's scepticism cut like a knife, all the more because he couldn't deny it. He had to admit that the thought of beating Marcus that way, of inheriting what his half-brother most wanted, had seemed at the time to present itself as the most perfect form of revenge.

At the time.

'How can it not be what you wanted?' Alyse challenged. 'When your mother tried everything she could to get your father to acknowledge you, year after year? When you say yourself that you worked so hard—made your fortune with the hope that he would recognise you as his son, or at least know that you existed. Well, didn't you?'

'Yes.'

He was not going to deny it. That had been how he had thought, what he had wanted. It all seemed so long ago now.

'I wanted that.' Or thought he'd wanted it. He'd lived so long with the emptiness inside him that he'd thought he'd finally found a way to fill it.

'And do you want this child?' Lightly, she touched her body, fingertips resting on where the baby—*his baby*—must lie, tiny as yet, and already turning his life inside out, changing things so totally. 'Do you?'

'Damn you to hell, yes!'

He might not know how to be a father, but there was one thing he knew for sure and that was that this baby—his child—would never feel unwanted as he had done. He would always be there for it, and he would never, ever turn away from it. He would be the best damned father he knew how to be.

'Because it will give you everything you ever wanted?'

'Yes.'

Too late, he realised that his response could be interpreted so very differently from the way he'd meant it. She wouldn't believe it if he tried to tell her what he really meant. And who would blame her?

Silently, Dario cursed the way that Alyse had discovered his father's letter before he had had time to resolve the problem. He'd been on his way out to talk to Henry just now. To tell him that he wanted no part of his scheming and manipulating. He wanted to put all that behind him so that he could move on. Move on into the sort of world that offered a future instead of tying him to the past.

'No,' Alyse said now, her fine-boned face set into a cold, determined expression, her green eyes hooded, hiding every emotion from him. Her hand still rested on her belly, but it seemed to Dario that this time the gesture had changed from one that was a gentle indication to a sign of protection, defending her child against the world.

Against him? It was like a knife going through him.

'No. Now you claim this child—*now* you "do family."' Her voice rang with defiance, with rejection. 'Well, there's something you need to know. I will never, ever let my baby be used as a bargaining tool, as your father did with you. As he wants to do with it now. Oh, don't look so horrified, Dario. I'm not going to deny you access, if that's what you want.'

'If I— Can you doubt it?'

'Oh, yes, I can.' Alyse's eyes blazed green fire into his, openly challenging him to stop her, to contradict her. 'You don't do family, remember.'

'I was a fool when I said that,' Dario put in sharply but

either she didn't hear him or she deliberately ignored his interjection, going on with her declaration as if she had determined to get it all out and no one was to stop her or divert her from what she had to say.

'But I'll do it for you. You can see your child—have access to your child whenever you want. But you can't have me.'

Dario's shoulders had just begun to relax, some of the tension leaving his body, when she hit him with that last comment, slapping him in the face with it so that his thoughts reeled.

You can't have me.

The words sounded like the slamming of a door. A sound he knew only too well. It was like going back all those years, to when he was fifteen. When he had stood on the doorstep of Kavanaugh House, pleading—begging—for his father's acknowledgement, for Henry's help for his dying mother. And the door had shut in his face.

...even as your ex-wife. The words she'd flung at him echoed round in his head. He'd thought she was testing him, seeing how much he was committed to caring for this child. He'd never actually thought that she was already seeing herself as his ex—and their marriage as being over.

'You can't have me,' Alyse repeated. 'I want more than this. More than the "allowance" you give me.'

'If you want more, you can have it. How much...?'

She didn't hesitate, not for a second, and he knew what she was going to say before she'd even opened her mouth. He thought that he'd seen the face of rejection before, but never, ever like this.

'I don't want an income—I don't want maintenance. I don't want anything from you. All that money you paid off for my mother and father.'

'I could afford it—and it was worth it...'

And it would have bought him what he wanted—his father's recognition. But was that worth everything he had paid for it?

It *was* worth it. Alyse wrapped her arms around her body to stop herself from falling apart. He had spoken of their marriage in the past. It seemed he had already put it behind him. Something she had struggled with and so far found totally impossible.

'I want to do this...'

'But I don't want it! In fact, what I really wish I could do is to pay you some of it back. You gave me—us so much when you paid off the gambling debts, got Marcus off our backs...'

'It was in the agreement.'

'But I can't just take everything. I doubt I'll ever be able to repay you what you gave us— I'll always be in your debt.'

'And did you not think that you have already paid off your *debt* already?'

Dario's mouth twisted around the word *debt* as if he was tasting poison.

'Don't you think that what you've already done to fulfil our contract will count as repayment against whatever "bill" you think you owe me?'

No, she couldn't answer that one honestly. Not when he stood so tall and dark between her and the window, a black oppressive silhouette looming over her.

'Why would I think that?' she hedged.

'Well, if you're reckoning up—if you really want to balance the money paid out against the benefits received, then—'

'Then our marriage, short as it is—*was*—has to reduce my debt just a bit?'

She gagged on the words, unable to believe he actually thought that way. That he would balance their days—their nights—together against the money she had cost him in some appalling reckoning of gains and loss. But, of course, he hadn't got what he'd wanted, had he? His father, cold, calculating, scheming, was not likely to pay out in any way when Dario hadn't come up with everything he demanded.

Like father, like son?

'Does it? So tell me, Dario, what do you think I might have paid off—how much has my bill been reduced, do you think?'

He didn't answer her, but then she didn't expect him to. His scowl might have stopped a lesser woman in her tracks, but the truth was that Alyse couldn't have halted if she'd tried. The deadly combination of pain and anger had made her tongue run away with her, no chance of reining it in or holding it back.

'So let me see—we've been married…what…? Four months? Making lo—having sex, what? Ten times a week? More? Even at that estimate, that's over one hundred and fifty times. So how much have I earned? How much per night?'

'I don't think like that.'

'Well, perhaps now it's time that you did. Because I need to know. How much have I paid off my debts to you, hmm? Surely you can give me some idea?' The pain was too much, burning like acid through her heart. 'I mean, what do you normally pay your whores?'

If she had tossed something foul right in his face then his head couldn't have gone any further back and, before his eyelids dropped over his eyes, she saw that they had lost all colour, his pupils just black slits.

'For your information, I don't associate with whores—no matter how much or little they cost me. Every woman I've ever been with has known how valued she was, great or small, and all—*all*—were happy with the way things were. But you...'

Astonishingly, he seemed to have lost control of his breathing. Something choked him to a halt, making him shake his head savagely, pull in a raw, ragged breath before he could go on.

'You come way too expensive. You cost far too much.'

You cost far too much.

Alyse felt sure that he must hear the sound of her hopes shattering and falling into pieces all around her. It was only now that she acknowledged her wild, foolish, naive dreams. Dreams that she had barely really recognised. It was only now that, just for a minute, she allowed herself to acknowledge that she had actually imagined that he might have said he didn't want to let her go.

But she'd forgotten the real truth about their marriage. Forgotten that to Dario it was purely a business deal and that that was all he wanted from her. Her place at his side, her body in his bed. Her name on the certificates that would make his father fulfil his promises. No commitment, no feelings except for sexual passion, no emotions creeping in to spoil the conditions that had been part of the contract.

She had dodged the real issue—that Dario didn't love her. And not loving her obviously meant that he wasn't prepared to put up with this change in their circumstances. He'd made that plain in that flat, cold statement.

You come way too expensive.

He'd warned her, hadn't he? Told her straight. So why should it hurt so much, tear at her like this to realise that he'd meant it? Because when had Dario ever said anything that he didn't truly mean?

'You're so right. You couldn't afford me now—and it would never be worth it, not for me. I want more than a man who marries me for what I can bring him…'

'I *wanted* you!'

Was that fury or accusation in his voice? Either way, it was too little too late.

'I want more than that too. I've spent my life being used by other people and I can't let it happen any more. My parents used me to get them out of the mess they were in—either through marriage to Marcus, or then to you. Your father used you, played you like a pro… Marcus would have used me if he could—to get his father's approval, the damned family home—and you…you…'

She choked up, tears thickening in her throat, blocking her from speaking. And if there was anything that could have stopped her from going on, if there had been any sort of chance for them, then if Dario had spoken now it might actually have had some effect.

But instead he stood there, dark and silent, blue eyes clouded and opaque, no trace of any emotion on his face. He had no comeback to offer her. There was no chance of any denial, any protest—fool that she was to even hope for it. He was taking everything she was throwing at him and putting up no defence. Probably because he thought he didn't need to defend himself—or because he knew that there was no way he could even try to deny what was the real truth behind his actions.

'Well, it stops here,' she managed, no longer needing to fight to keep her voice calm and cold. That happened all on its own as she acknowledged the way that Dario had not argued against the truth. 'It stops now and it's never going to happen again.'

Had he turned to ice? she wondered in the frozen silence that greeted the end of her outburst, the final words falling in a desperate cry into the emptiness around them. Had the coldness of his life, his thoughts—his heart—finally reached out and enclosed him so that he couldn't move or say a word? But then what could he say? He'd made no move to deny her accusations, offered no expression of feeling—of any sort of feeling—but instead had just stood there, still and mute, and never tried to interrupt or say anything.

And now that she had fallen silent he still wasn't going to speak. Or move. Or act in any way.

It stops now and it's never going to happen again. Her own words came back to haunt her, sounding like the final full stop, the death knell to everything. He wasn't going to even try to protest, to change anything.

It stops now...

'Yes.'

Just one word, low and flat—Dario's only response. Nothing more.

He'd barely spoken when there was a tap at the door that still stood open from the moment that Dario had walked in, finding her with the pregnancy test in her hand...and those appalling letters in the drawer.

'Excuse me...'

José, the chauffeur, who had been sitting in the car for Dario to come back and give him instructions to drive him somewhere. But he'd obviously decided that, having waited so long, he might as well make use of his time by bringing up the cases they had brought back from Tuscany. He deposited them on the floor now, hers and Dario's standing side by side.

'Shall I put these in...?'

'No.'

It was Alyse who spoke, rushing in while Dario still stood as if he had never said that single word.

'No, José—will you please take my case back down to the car and then—' She glanced at Dario, feeling now that her own face must be as set and stiff as his. She could feel her jaw muscles aching with the battle for control, her eyes not focusing quite right.

'I assume you'll let José drive me?'

'Where are you going?'

Could he sound any less interested? The question had no intonation in it whatsoever. No trace of any sort of feeling.

'I don't know yet. But I'll let you know.'

That brought a tiny touch of reaction, his eyes narrowing sharply as he frowned a question.

'I promised you that you'd have access to our child,' she told him. 'I'll keep that promise.'

It was as much as she could manage. She couldn't take any more. So, determined not to break down, to risk turning back in case the sight of him standing there took all the strength from her and tempted her to turn back, she spun round on her heel and marched from the room, leaving José to follow with her bag.

If she so much as hesitated, if she turned round just once, Dario told himself, then perhaps he might find some words—might find something to say to make her change her mind. But what words would do that? What could he say except that one single syllable—that 'Yes' that had been all he could offer before?

Because what else was there to say? He couldn't refute her accusations of wanting her because he believed she would give him what he hungered for. They were all true. In the beginning, at least. But the fact that things had changed did nothing to reduce the way they had been there in his thoughts, driving him on, driving him to her.

He couldn't contradict her declaration that this stopped now—and it never happened again. It was what he wanted. It was how it should be. No more lies. Never again.

So *yes* was the only possible answer. Unless he could find something to put in its place. Because he had to find something or the future was going to be impossible to face.

But it was only as the silence of the empty apartment settled down around him and the rooms seemed to echo with the hollowness of space that he realised just what had gone and how much he had lost.

CHAPTER TWELVE

'WHAT ARE YOU doing here?'

Alyse couldn't quite accept that she had actually opened the door to Dario. She didn't even know that he remembered she had a friend called Rose, let alone knew where Rose's flat might be. When she had walked out on him, this had been the only place she could think of to go to, to hide out there, trying to work out just how to rebuild her life and face a future that had suddenly turned into an arid desert. The last thing she had expected was that Dario would track her down and come to her here.

'How did you know where to find me?'

'I thought about trying your parents' house first. But then, of course, I realised you'd not go back there again—' he almost laughed at her response, the expression of rejection that must show in her eyes '—no matter how desperate you were.'

Dario's voice was low and husky and he looked rough, his jaw darkened by a day's growth of beard, shadows like bruises under his eyes. She'd thought that she looked washed out, several nights without sleep showing on her face when she'd looked in the mirror this morning, but quite frankly Dario looked worse.

'So I asked José where he'd taken you.'

Thinking only of getting away, fighting nausea, almost

all of her energy focused on keeping the tears, ever at the back of her eyes, from slipping to her cheeks, she'd asked the chauffeur to drive her to Rose's office. Obviously, Dario had followed the trail from there.

'I told Rose not to let on...'

'I know—but I managed to persuade her.' Even the half-voltage rough-edged smile he turned on reminded her of just how persuasive Dario could be when he wanted. 'I told her I had something important for you.'

'You did? I didn't leave anything behind.'

'No, this is something I want to give you.'

He lifted one hand, showing her the large document file he held in it.

'No...'

Alyse had to admit it, her heart had lifted just a tiny bit, felt a weak little twist of hope when she had seen him, but now it dropped right down into the pit of her stomach, making her feel horribly nauseous as she took two instinctive steps backwards, her eyes fixed on that file. She could only imagine the one thing that had brought him here like this—that duty he felt towards his child, and to her as the mother of that baby. And she couldn't bear that that was all.

'Can I come in?' His diffidence surprised her but she could hardly leave him standing in the hallway so she beckoned him in, only to find that he was holding out the file as he came towards her.

'I don't want it!'

Alyse found she was shaking her head more violently now, her hair flying around her face as she did so.

'You've done enough, more than enough, already.'

A wave of his hand dismissed it as only a hugely wealthy man could dismiss such a huge amount.

'Didn't you listen?' she managed, holding her body stiff and straight so that he couldn't see the way she was quaking inside, not knowing if she could handle this. 'Whatever it is, I don't want it.'

It had torn her apart to leave him, to see him, she believed, for the last time. Now he had come after her, come back into her life and even if it was just for the shortest possible time she knew that parting would have to be done again. She had barely got through it the first time. She didn't know how she would do it again.

'I can't cost you anything more.'

'Oh, but you can. You have to.'

It wasn't anger that had affected him so badly, Alyse realised with a sense of shock. There wasn't fury in his eyes but something else, something that looked disturbingly like pain. But what had put that there?

'I can't…' she began again then broke off in consternation as he pulled a document from the file, held it out to her. 'What?'

Dario said nothing but continued to hold the papers out to her. Slowly, she reached out, took them, forced her eyes to focus, read partway, then, unable to believe what she had seen, went back and read again.

'What?' she repeated, unable to get her head round this, unable to think any further. 'Dario—this is…?'

'The deeds to the Villa D'Oro,' Dario supplied when she couldn't. 'The legal transfer of the property from me to you.'

So now she understood just why he had said she cost too much. He was actually handing over his home—the home he had bought in his mother's memory—the home that held the only connection he had to his family—to her. She could only begin to guess at what that had cost him, in all senses of the word.

'You can't…'

'I can and I have. What do I need with a house that big?

I would only rattle around in it. But you—and the child—you'll need a family home.'

Alyse had thought that her head was spinning in shock already but it was when he said the words 'family home', the dark intonation he put on them, that something exploded in her mind, sending her reeling away across the room, needing to put a hand out to the wall to support her.

'Kavanaugh House...' It was a strangled gasp. Could he part with the villa because he already had the Kavanaugh family home tied up legally safe and sound? 'Your father...'

Dario had known this was coming but he still hated to hear those words on her lips, to know that his father's malign influence still reached this far.

'No,' he said, putting every ounce of conviction into the single word. 'Damn it to hell, Alyse—*no*. He has not had any part in this for a long time. Not since the day I married you.'

She needed more than that, he could see. And he was happy to give it to her.

'I'll admit that when I heard how Henry wanted you as his daughter-in-law, that he would delight in the connection to your family so much that he wanted to reward Marcus—give him a huge part of his inheritance early—I was determined to wreck those plans. And then when Henry...' he would never honour that man with the name of *father* ever again '...when he sent me that letter—offering me his recognition, the acknowledgement of my being his son, if I was the one who married you...'

He pulled out another document, one that Alyse recognised this time. The letters from Henry Kavanaugh telling Dario how he would be rewarded if he presented the old man with first a daughter-in-law with a title and then a grandchild.

'I was tempted, I admit—' Dario shook his dark head as if in disgust at his own weakness. 'But after our wedding I no longer wanted any of that. Or anything to do with him.'

There was still doubt in her eyes; she was still not convinced. But he had to try. His father was dead to him—the only thing worth fighting for was this.

He held out his hand towards her, gesturing towards the letters.

'Give them to me.'

She seemed frozen to the spot so he reached out and took them from her nerveless hands. With several brisk, sharp movements, he tore the paper in two and then in two again, ripping it over and over until it was in tiny irreparable pieces that he tossed to the floor so that they lay like confetti around her feet.

'But I don't understand.' She looked as dazed as if they had been something cold and shocking that had hit her in the face.

How could she understand when he didn't fully comprehend what was happening himself? He only knew that when she had taken herself and the baby—his baby, his family—away from this relationship that something had shattered deep inside. He had hated the way she had talked about needing to repay him, the way she had equated every night in his bed with something that was part of what she owed him, something that could be equated with money—the cost for every time they had been together.

What do you normally pay your whores?

The terrible words swung round and round in his head, threatening to destroy him in a way that was far, far worse than the rejection his father had ever turned on him, the way that Marcus had made sure that the door was slammed shut in his face. He had been able to survive those wounds and live on. The way he had felt since that day when she had walked out had left him fearing that this injury might just be fatal.

'Dario...that letter would have given you everything you wanted. Your father— No?' She broke off on the question as he shook his head violently, stamping the shreds of the letter under his foot as he did so.

'No—damn it to hell, no!'

Black fury was raging inside at his father, and at the way that man could still reach out and touch his life, make Alyse feel this way, make the woman he...

It was as if a huge sheet of glass had suddenly descended, cutting him off from reality, silencing the rest of the world and enclosing him so there was only Alyse and himself in existence.

Only himself and the woman he loved.

'No.'

It was all that he could manage. The only thing he could say. The only thing she had to believe.

'He gives me nothing. Nothing at all.'

'But he does...'

Alyse couldn't find a way to get a grip on what was happening. The letters that Dario had just destroyed completely had told him that, after all these years of rejection and loneliness, he could be recognised as Henry Kavanaugh's son.

'He'll acknowledge you...'

So was he prepared to give that up? Give up the dream he'd held for his mother's sake? And why?

'He'd accept me only because of what I bring him—not because of who I am.'

And she could understand that, couldn't she?

A shocking realisation hit home and had her shaking in despair, unable to accept what he'd done.

'How can you give me Villa D'Oro—your family home—unless...'

'You think I'd only part with the villa because I now have possession of the Kavanaughs'...'

Dario's voice failed him and he could only toss his dark head in rejection of even the thought.

'You couldn't be more wrong. I have to give you Villa D'Oro because I can't live there. Not without you. If you're not there it's not a home—and most definitely not a family home. Without you, it's just an address, a place with no soul, no heart. You are the heart of that place. You turned it from a house into a home, and without you it will always be empty.'

Something in her face gave him the nerve to move forward, reach out a hand to her. But only to reach it out. He didn't yet take her fingers in his, knowing there was still more that had to be said.

'As for Kavanaugh, I want nothing from him. I need nothing he can give me. Whatever he offers, the cost is just not worth it. I'm not a Kavanaugh. I'm an Olivero. My mother's name—and the name I hope my child will bear too.'

Unbelievably, it seemed that Dario's emotions were running away with him. For the first time Alyse actually saw him lose control, struggle with composure, fight for the ability to go on.

'And this man dares to want you—*you*!—only as the mother of his grandchild, the inheritance of a title. You are so much more than that. Worth an infinity more than that. And our child will never, ever be known only for what he or she brings to the status of our family.'

'Our family?'

It caught on her tongue, choking her. It threatened to stop her breathing because of what it said. It said so much more than she could ever have imagined or dreamed. And had he really included her in there too—in his *family*?

'We don't have a family,' she managed through a mouth that was painfully dry so that her tongue seemed stiff as a piece of wood. 'All we have is a business arrangement, one where you paid for what you wanted...'

She couldn't go on, despair crushing her lungs so that she couldn't catch any breath.

'What I wanted?' Dario echoed the words as if they were poisonous. 'Damn you, no.'

She couldn't understand the reason for the rawness in his tone, the harshness of his voice.

'You paid for me in your bed—you...'

The words were snatched from her as her head spun in disbelief as he pulled out another document. This one she recognised when he thrust it at her wildly. She didn't need to read it. It was the pre-nuptial agreement she had signed before their marriage. Was it really only four months? Sixteen short weeks? It felt like a lifetime ago.

'I know you never read it fully. So read it now, damn you—read it properly.'

It was almost impossible to follow his command as the words danced and squirmed before her eyes. She could barely take it in but she knew that she had to. Every expression on his face told her that—the burn of those blue eyes, the patches of white where the skin was drawn tight and hard around his mouth and eyes, etched against the side of his nose.

So she read it once. Then read it over again because she couldn't believe what she was reading. She hadn't signed this—had she?

But there at the bottom of the page was her signature, along with the black scrawl that was Dario's name. Making it legal and binding—to him.

Because, apart from the formality of the wedding, the only things that really mattered in this document were the things it locked *Dario* into doing.

She had believed that Dario had demanded that she marry him to share his bed—to become his lover—and that those were the conditions that he had written into the pre-nuptial agreement he'd had drawn up. That basically he had bought her, body and soul, for the price of the rescue package for her parents. A hugely expensive rescue package for which he'd been justified in demanding a very high price.

But not the price she'd thought he'd insisted on.

'You—you only wanted to *marry* me.' Her voice was filled with the shock of realisation. 'You didn't...'

The contract tied her only to marrying him, changing her name to his. He hadn't put down in writing that it was to be 'a proper marriage', one that meant she was to share his bed, share her body with him. She had thought, had believed, that he would make it a condition of his bailout package for her parents that she had to sleep with him, but that was not the case.

'I married you because I wanted you. Yes, I wanted to see my father and my damned half-brother defeated in their foul little plan. I wanted to make sure that Marcus didn't get his filthy hands on you. But no, I didn't want to buy you like some very expensive prostitute. I wanted you in my bed—but you had to come there of your own choice. After that, I wanted a willing woman in my bed. I've never forced a woman in my life and I certainly didn't intend to start with my wife, even if you only married me because I bought you. Because I paid off all your family's debts.'

'No...' She struggled to put any strength into the word but, looking into his face, seeing the dark intensity etched there, told her that she had to go on, had to make this so very clear. She couldn't bear to have him thinking anything else. 'I married you because I wanted you too. You were the one who insisted on marriage… You did!'

She almost laughed as she caught the touch of shamefaced acknowledgement in his expression. But the laughter shrivelled as she thought of the significance of what that expression meant.

'Yes, I thought that the only way I would win my father's recognition was by marrying you—but that delusion was shattered on the day of our wedding, when he didn't even trouble to attend or even acknowledge my invitation. It was all what he wanted, how he wanted it—and nothing more.'

I don't do family. In her head Alyse could hear those words as he had spoken them outside the church. The terrible, bitter disillusionment that had sounded in them then.

And, even as she thought it, she heard him echo the words from her own thoughts.

'I don't…do family.'

'I know…'

It was a sigh of resignation and acceptance. But then that sigh was caught up, cut off between one breath and another as she paused to think, to register that he hadn't said exactly what she'd believed. Not quite.

'What? What did you say?'

For a couple of uneasy seconds she thought that he wasn't going to respond to her challenge. But then a slight brusque inclination of his head dismissed whatever second thoughts he was having.

'I don't know how to do family,' he said, low and tight. 'But, with you, I found I wanted to try.'

She couldn't believe it. She had to have heard wrong. There was no way he could have said…

But looking into those blue eyes that she loved so much she could see the shadows that clouded them. She could hear the rawness in his voice that threatened to pull his words apart, unravelling them totally.

'When...?' It was barely a whisper.

'The first night at the villa, and ever after that.' His eyes held hers, burning into her, willing her, begging her to believe. 'I could have told you then. I should have told you—but I knew then I would never want to let you go,' Dario said and there was no doubting the depth of conviction in his tone, the shadowed certainty in his face. 'I just didn't know what to call it.'

'And—and now?' Her voice was just a thin thread of sound but she knew the moment he caught it, saw the stunning change in his face. It was as if someone had lit him up from within, but at the same time he didn't dare quite reveal all that was inside him.

'And now I'm admitting that it's love. I'm in love with you. I love you so much that I hate the way you'd even think I'd only pay to have you in my bed. I need you in my life—I love you so much that I want you to be with me for ever. Want you as my love, my wife, the mother of my child.'

'But you—' she began then broke off as he moved forward, taking her hands, holding them tight against his chest.

'Don't say it—' he begged and she knew the words hung unspoken between them. 'Don't remind me of how stupid I was. How ignorant and unable to recognise... I didn't know what a family was. I only knew that it had to be more than what my father and my mother made of a blood family. That there had to be more than the blood ties that bound me—unwillingly—to Henry and to Marcus.'

'They're no family to you!' Alyse interjected sharply,

unable to bear the thought of the way his so-called family had treated him.

'I know—and I didn't want them to be either. I wanted the sort of family that you had. The sort of family where your father cares enough to risk jail to save your mother from breaking down completely. And where you were prepared to sign away a part of your life to help them both. Dear God, but I wanted that.'

'Really?'

'Really.' It was firm and strong, totally sure. 'I'd always vaguely understood that the appeal of a family—a real family—the reason for it being was a very special closeness, a need of each other and caring for each other. You can't order it, you can't buy it, no matter how much you pay—it has to grow and become real. It started to grow the first time we made love. And it was there between us that day on the terrace.'

'It was there before that,' Alyse said softly. 'It was there when you cared for me—when you nursed me through the migraine—for better, for worse.'

Dario's smile was wry, softly reminiscent.

'That led to today—to the baby. And now...'

His hand slid down over her belly, curved protectively over the spot where his baby nestled, tiny as yet, but growing into a real child, a person, a member of their family.

'Now, our child will be loved for who it is, not because of anything it brings to our marriage except itself. Just as I love you for who you are and I always will. I don't know how to be a father but I'll be the best damn *papà* I can be.'

Suddenly his voice dropped, fell from the declaration he'd made into a raw and aching whisper.

'I still don't know how to do family. I just know I want to try. With you.'

I just know I want to try. With you. What braver, greater

declaration could there be? How could she ask for anything more?

'And I want to try too,' she said, her voice deep with conviction. 'With you as the man I love. The father of my child.'

Alyse leaned forward, offered him her mouth, and knew the soaring sense of true happiness, true fulfilment as he took it in the longest, most loving kiss she had ever experienced. She moved into his arms, feeling safe and secure there and knowing she would never, ever want to leave them.

'Let me tell you something,' she whispered, the softness of her love and her happiness in her smile. 'I don't really know how to do this sort of family either. Not one where I'm the mother and you—my love, my husband, my future—are the father. But I do know one thing. We'll learn together. We'll make a real family. And that's all that anyone could ever ask for.'

* * * * *

MILLS & BOON®
Hardback – April 2015

ROMANCE

The Billionaire's Bridal Bargain	Lynne Graham
At the Brazilian's Command	Susan Stephens
Carrying the Greek's Heir	Sharon Kendrick
The Sheikh's Princess Bride	Annie West
His Diamond of Convenience	Maisey Yates
Olivero's Outrageous Proposal	Kate Walker
The Italian's Deal for I Do	Jennifer Hayward
Virgin's Sweet Rebellion	Kate Hewitt
The Millionaire and the Maid	Michelle Douglas
Expecting the Earl's Baby	Jessica Gilmore
Best Man for the Bridesmaid	Jennifer Faye
It Started at a Wedding...	Kate Hardy
Just One Night?	Carol Marinelli
Meant-To-Be Family	Marion Lennox
The Soldier She Could Never Forget	Tina Beckett
The Doctor's Redemption	Susan Carlisle
Wanted: Parents for a Baby!	Laura Iding
His Perfect Bride?	Louisa Heaton
Twins on the Way	Janice Maynard
The Nanny Plan	Sarah M. Anderson

0315 GEN STD HB

MILLS & BOON®
Large Print – April 2015

ROMANCE

Taken Over by the Billionaire	Miranda Lee
Christmas in Da Conti's Bed	Sharon Kendrick
His for Revenge	Caitlin Crews
A Rule Worth Breaking	Maggie Cox
What The Greek Wants Most	Maya Blake
The Magnate's Manifesto	Jennifer Hayward
To Claim His Heir by Christmas	Victoria Parker
Snowbound Surprise for the Billionaire	Michelle Douglas
Christmas Where They Belong	Marion Lennox
Meet Me Under the Mistletoe	Cara Colter
A Diamond in Her Stocking	Kandy Shepherd

HISTORICAL

Strangers at the Altar	Marguerite Kaye
Captured Countess	Ann Lethbridge
The Marquis's Awakening	Elizabeth Beacon
Innocent's Champion	Meriel Fuller
A Captain and a Rogue	Liz Tyner

MEDICAL

It Started with No Strings...	Kate Hardy
One More Night with Her Desert Prince...	Jennifer Taylor
Flirting with Dr Off-Limits	Robin Gianna
From Fling to Forever	Avril Tremayne
Dare She Date Again?	Amy Ruttan
The Surgeon's Christmas Wish	Annie O'Neil

MILLS & BOON®
Hardback – May 2015

ROMANCE

The Sheikh's Secret Babies	Lynne Graham
The Sins of Sebastian Rey-Defoe	Kim Lawrence
At Her Boss's Pleasure	Cathy Williams
Captive of Kadar	Trish Morey
The Marakaios Marriage	Kate Hewitt
Craving Her Enemy's Touch	Rachael Thomas
The Greek's Pregnant Bride	Michelle Smart
Greek's Last Redemption	Caitlin Crews
The Pregnancy Secret	Cara Colter
A Bride for the Runaway Groom	Scarlet Wilson
The Wedding Planner and the CEO	Alison Roberts
Bound by a Baby Bump	Ellie Darkins
Always the Midwife	Alison Roberts
Midwife's Baby Bump	Susanne Hampton
A Kiss to Melt Her Heart	Emily Forbes
Tempted by Her Italian Surgeon	Louisa George
Daring to Date Her Ex	Annie Claydon
The One Man to Heal Her	Meredith Webber
The Sheikh's Pregnancy Proposal	Fiona Brand
Minding Her Boss's Business	Janice Maynard

MILLS & BOON®
Large Print – May 2015

ROMANCE

The Secret His Mistress Carried	Lynne Graham
Nine Months to Redeem Him	Jennie Lucas
Fonseca's Fury	Abby Green
The Russian's Ultimatum	Michelle Smart
To Sin with the Tycoon	Cathy Williams
The Last Heir of Monterrato	Andie Brock
Inherited by Her Enemy	Sara Craven
Taming the French Tycoon	Rebecca Winters
His Very Convenient Bride	Sophie Pembroke
The Heir's Unexpected Return	Jackie Braun
The Prince She Never Forgot	Scarlet Wilson

HISTORICAL

Marriage Made in Money	Sophia James
Chosen by the Lieutenant	Anne Herries
Playing the Rake's Game	Bronwyn Scott
Caught in Scandal's Storm	Helen Dickson
Bride for a Knight	Margaret Moore

MEDICAL

Playing the Playboy's Sweetheart	Carol Marinelli
Unwrapping Her Italian Doc	Carol Marinelli
A Doctor by Day...	Emily Forbes
Tamed by the Renegade	Emily Forbes
A Little Christmas Magic	Alison Roberts
Christmas with the Maverick Millionaire	Scarlet Wilson

MILLS & BOON®

Why shop at millsandboon.co.uk?

Each year, thousands of romance readers find their perfect read at millsandboon.co.uk. That's because we're passionate about bringing you the very best romantic fiction. Here are some of the advantages of shopping at www.millsandboon.co.uk:

* **Get new books first**—you'll be able to buy your favourite books one month before they hit the shops

* **Get exclusive discounts**—you'll also be able to buy our specially created monthly collections, with up to 50% off the RRP

* **Find your favourite authors**—latest news, interviews and new releases for all your favourite authors and series on our website, plus ideas for what to try next

* **Join in**—once you've bought your favourite books, don't forget to register with us to rate, review and join in the discussions

Visit **www.millsandboon.co.uk**
for all this and more today!